The Blind Tailor's Daughter

NELL HARTE

Disclaimer

This story is a work of fiction, any resemblance to people is purely coincidence. All places, names, events, businesses, etc. are used in a fictional manner. All characters are from the imagination of the author.

Table of Contents

Chapter One

York, Winter 1863

Drizzling rain hardened to ice on the shadowed cobbles of the city, as the bells of York Minster tolled the night warning to those who were not yet warm in their beds or safe behind closed doors and candlelight. For the beggars and vagrants, refuge was sought wherever it could be found, those lost souls accompanied only by the mumble of their own voices, praying to be alive when morning came. Or not... for it was a hard life, made all the harder without family and friends to lean upon, and not two coins to rub together.

But above the sea-green exterior of Acklam & Sons, the amber glow that spilled out onto the ice-slicked street below could have flowed from the very hearts of the joyful family within, who were in the midst of a celebration.

"Six-and-ten is a noble age," Bonnie Acklam's mother, Clara, announced, as she produced something from behind her back. She set the gift upon the worn kitchen table, where the Acklam family of four shared all of their meals together, never wanting for much.

Bonnie gasped at the sight of the delicacy, her eyes as wide as the plate upon which the treat had been served. "This is too much, Mama! The neighbours will call us wasteful if they were to get a whiff of this!"

It was a cake, dripping white icing. A pound cake, all in honour of her sixteenth year upon this Earth.

"Don't you worry about the neighbours, lass. Let 'em be jealous. It's not so often that I get to spoil me eldest girl," her mother replied with a wink, her voice still carrying a hint of her humbler origins as a dairy maid in the wilds of North Yorkshire.

Bonnie's younger sister, Alice, licked her lips hungrily. At twelve years of age, nothing delighted Alice as much as the promise of sugar, for though the Acklam family were reasonably well-off, they were not frivolous. They knew how fortunate they were when every winter brought frozen bodies in doorways, and the lines at the churches grew longer each year, when hot soup and bread was being offered to those in need.

As much as they could, the Acklam family shared their good fortune, making charitable donations and giving what they did not need to the poor, but it would never be enough to remedy the great plague of poverty that seemed to blight every city and town, and not just in Yorkshire.

"Might I have some?" Alice asked eagerly.

Clara chuckled and turned back to the stove to stir the thick, meaty stew that bubbled merrily. "When your pa comes up and you've eaten all your dinner—then, you can have some. Don't want you spoilin' your appetites."

"Shall I fetch him?" Bonnie said, rising from her seat.

Her skirt and petticoats rustled as she moved toward the door, her ribs aching from the corset that she had only recently begun to wear.

Yet, she tried not to complain, for the same reason she felt a touch guilty about the cake: she was lucky.

Clara did not look up from the pot on the stove. "Don't trouble him if you can help it, but see if he can't give you a notion of when he might be done. I don't want this stew thickenin' too much more, else it'll be like porridge."

"Yes, Mama." Bonnie swept out of the warm apartments and down a draughty stairwell, where the January wind whistled through hairline cracks in the wall.

She picked her skirts up as she went, terrified of tripping and falling down the steep staircase.

Her friends liked to tell horrifying tales of such tragedies, scaring one another silly, for imagined calamities were the only things that they had to worry themselves about.

In their warm residences, their bellies full, their hearts merry, their minds still innocent, they could take their time in growing up.

They were safe in the knowledge that they would likely always lead a sheltered existence.

At the bottom of the stairwell, a long hallway led to the front door, where the rain peppered the wood like a shy passer-by hoping to gain entry. Another door on the left opened out into *Acklam & Sons—Tailors and Dressmakers.*

An unusual combination of both arts in one shop, perfectly and famously articulated by Bonnie's beloved father: a gifted man and the son of the Acklam who had given the shop its name, though there were no more sons to carry it on.

Clara had almost died giving birth to Alice and, since then, they had not been blessed with more children, but if Clara or her husband, Bernard, minded, they did not show it.

Instead, they poured everything they possessed into nurturing their two daughters, ensuring they were educated, appreciative, and, most of all, kind.

"Papa?" Bonnie called out, as she swung open the door to the shop.

The shop had always appeared eerie to her, once it was devoid of customers and the lights were extinguished, leaving only the ghoulish shape of mannequins, dressed and ready for a ball. Bonnie could never shrug away the feeling that they moved of their own volition, creeping towards her as if they sought her flesh-and-blood existence for themselves.

She hurried through the gloom, illuminated only by the streetlamps beyond the leaded windows, until she reached the workshop at the rear. The door stuttered for a moment as she tried to open it; the hinges swollen. Finally, with a reluctant wheeze, the door gave, sending her stumbling into her father's familiar domain.

Her father, hunched over his work in the farthest corner with his back to her, did not seem to notice the intrusion.

His fingertips, pinching a needle, moved with the grace of a ballerina, looping the thread in and out of a cascading reem of red silk, the colour of garnet. A bold choice of colour that Bonnie appreciated, wishing that, one day, she might be daring enough to wear such a gown to a ball or a gathering.

Of course, she would need to be invited to one first, but her father was never short on invitations to special occasions; he just never attended, seeing no reason to when his work spoke for itself.

Indeed, after every illustrious soirée, whether it took place in York or London or Manchester or Bath, he found himself inundated with requests, each lady and gentleman vying for priority with as much money as they could reasonably muster.

But that was the mystery and appeal of her father's work: he accepted commissions only from those he chose to, refusing to buckle underneath the pressure of a thousand demands.

The Acklam family could have been exceedingly wealthy, had he wanted them to be, but he was happy as long as his family had enough; he would not work himself to the bone for more than was necessary to be comfortable. Bonnie had always admired that about him.

Secretly pleased that her entrance had not been noticed, Bonnie lingered by the doorway, observing her father as he continued to work.

Other, finished masterpieces were hung upon mannequins or wrapped in pretty white boxes, tied with ribbons that were the same sea green as the shop's exterior, where they awaited collection from the errand boys and express riders who arrived each day.

The gentlemanly attire was pleasant to the eye, too, but Bonnie preferred to bask in the beauty of the intricate, exquisite gowns, revelling in the explosions of colour that brightened the otherwise plain workshop.

"Blast it all," her father muttered sharply, prompting Bonnie's heart to jump in her chest. He never spoke unkindly to her, never raised his voice to anyone, yet she had not mistaken the violence in his voice.

Bernard paused, setting down the needle and thread so he could bring the knuckles of his fingers to his eyes. He rubbed them, hissing in the back of his throat as if he was in pain.

A few moments later, he sat back on the worn, uncomfortable stool where he did all of his work—his wife and children had tried to insist upon a nice, wing-backed chair, but he had refused, explaining that "If I'm too at ease, I'll get nothing done." He stared up at the ceiling, narrowing and widening his eyes, blinking rapidly before resuming the vehement rubbing with his hooked knuckles.

"There's no time for this," he rasped at no one at all, for it appeared he still did not know he had company.

Returning his attention to his workbench, a horrified expression strained his still-handsome features, his fingertips fumbling across the dark green mats that caught stray fibres and severed filaments of thread. He closed one eye, huffing and puffing as he continued to skim his hands over the workbench, his demeanour growing more desperate with every passing second.

Has he lost his needle? Bonnie considered it to be the only explanation, and not so unusual; he was always losing needles and sending the girls out to purchase more from the haberdashery: a tiny shop, tucked away in the narrow lanes of the Shambles.

Bonnie loved being given the task, for walking through the Shambles made her feel as if she had been transported to a different century, her mind conjuring the sights and sounds of a bygone time when kings lopped off heads on a whim and feasted upon swans, holding medieval gatherings filled with smoke and mystery and gowns so ostentatious that the ladies could barely walk in them.

Bonnie's mother often told her that her daydreams were "ghoulish," but she preferred to think of it as being grateful for the current state of things—a country with an inspiring, venerable queen upon the throne who loved her husband and was dutiful to her subjects.

"The men will tell you otherwise, but women make for better monarchs," her mother had whispered to her one night. *"They've a more sensible head on their shoulders. That's why there are men who'll look for any excuse to call 'em hysterical. Don't want us women gettin' ideas above our station."*

The sentiment had stuck with Bonnie, giving her the—perhaps misguided—sense that she could achieve anything she set her mind to. What that might be, she was not yet sure, but she did know one thing: she would make something of herself, one day. *She* would be a woman to be celebrated, like Queen Victoria.

"Where is it?" her father hissed, drawing her out of the imagined streets of the Shambles and back into the gloomy workshop. His jaw clenched, a surprising curse of "Damn it all!" leaving his lips. Bonnie understood a second later, as he lifted his finger and put it in his mouth: he had found the needle.

Bonnie hurried to him. "Are you well, Papa? Did it prick you?"

Her father jolted as if she had leapt out of the shadows at him, his breath rasping from his lungs, his eyes wide in terror.

"It's me, Papa," she said quietly, panic bubbling through her veins as she noted his distress. She had not meant to scare him.

"I didn't know you were there," her father replied, after a moment; his breath slowing. "You gave me quite the fright. What have I told you about creeping up on poor souls?" He laughed, but it sounded forced, his eyes still wide to the whites.

"What's wrong, Papa?" Bonnie was no fool; she could feel the fear still emanating from him, his precious, gifted hands trembling. And she doubted it had anything to do with her sudden appearance.

He could not look her in the eyes. "I've got a gown that must be finished by the morning, and it's still in pieces. That's all, darling." He gestured to the door. "You go back upstairs and enjoy your birthday. Six-and-ten only happens once."

"All ages only happen once." Bonnie mustered a smile, trying not to let her worries get the better of her. If her father said it was just the stress of his work, it was her duty as his daughter to believe him.

Her father nodded, laughing faintly. "Quite right. I hear your mother made you a cake—have a slice and bring me one down in a while." He paused. "I'm sorry, but I'll have to stay in the workshop until this is done, though you must know I'd prefer to be up there, celebrating with my girls."

"I know, Papa." She put her arms around him.

He hugged her back with a ferocity that frightened her, for it was as if he was clinging to life itself, squeezing the air out of her lungs.

He must have realised he was holding her too tightly, as he slowly released her. "Go on now, and tell your mother I'm sorry, too. I hate to disappoint you all."

"You haven't disappointed us, Papa," Bonnie told him sadly. "We owe everything we have to you. I'll bring you the biggest slice of cake Mama will let me cut."

Her father flinched, confusing her. "Thank you, darling."

Pressing a kiss to his cheek, Bonnie turned and headed for the upstairs apartments, but as she reached the door that opened onto the interior hallway, she stopped and looked back. Her father must have mistaken the squeal of hinges for the door closing again, not realising she was still there, for as he sat upon his worn and rickety stool, he hunched over, holding his head in his hands, his shoulders shaking as if he were crying.

"What do I do?" he whispered to the gloom. "What in heaven's name am I to do?"

Bonnie slipped out as silently as she could, her heart thundering in her chest, tears pricking at her own eyes, for she knew her father; if something had brought him so low that he wept, it could not be anything good. Indeed, picturing the manner in which he had fumbled for his needle and rubbed his eyes as if he wanted to remove them from his skull entirely, she feared the very worst.

Chapter Two

At three o'clock in the morning, if the bells of York Minster were to be believed, Bonnie could no longer lie idly in her bed, worrying for the beloved father who had not yet surfaced from his suffocating lair. Crawling out from beneath the coverlets, listening to the soft, peaceful breathing of her sister in the next-door bed, Bonnie grabbed her dressing gown and threw it on as she slunk out of the bedchamber on tiptoes.

Passing through the kitchen, her gaze flitted toward the pot on the stove, and the half-circle on the table that had been wrapped in waxed paper: the remains of the stew and the cake, with plenty to spare.

Perhaps, he will have eaten something by now, she mused anxiously. Earlier in the evening, when she had taken a slice to her father, he had not taken so much as a bite. And when she had returned an hour later to collect the plate, it still had not been touched. Nor had the bowl of stew, which had congealed. As a man who abhorred being wasteful, the sight of that untouched bowl had terrified Bonnie far more than any curse word or strained insistence of all being well.

"Don't, darling," a soft, sad voice murmured, as Bonnie reached the door to the staircase.

Bonnie whirled around in alarm, spotting a shadow in the corner of the kitchen. She heard the scratch and hiss of a match being struck, carrying the stinging smell of sulphur to her nostrils. A moment later, a candle wick burst into life, illuminating the tired and pale face of Bonnie's mother.

"I thought I'd see if he'd eaten his cake yet," Bonnie said limply, her heart aching at the haunting vision of her mother, sitting in that darkened corner as if she was holding a vigil.

"He hasn't," her mother replied. "Just let him work, darling."

Bonnie frowned. "Is William with him?"

"No, he is alone."

"Should someone not fetch William?" Despite the hour, Bonnie was ready to fulfil the task, for if her father needed assistance, then it seemed only sensible that he should have his apprentice with him. It might even be a worthwhile education in how to complete a gown with time running out.

Her mother got up, the dancing shadows of the candle deepening the hollows around her eyes. "Your father doesn't want him sent for."

"Whyever not?" Bonnie's hand reached for the door handle.

Her mother sighed. "Because he has said so."

"And when have you ever done something because "Papa said so," if it was utter nonsense?" Fear held Bonnie's lungs in a winching vice, her throat tightening as her worries plumed, spreading into something monstrous that slithered through her body, tar-black and just as cloying.

"Just... let him be, Bonnie."

But Bonnie could not. She would not. "Very well, if no one will summon William, then I'll offer my services to Papa." She wrenched open the door. "I know enough to be of use."

As Bonnie headed down the stairs at a clip, her mother followed, moving as slowly as someone sentenced to death. A weight of resignation turned her mother's every footstep leaden, and like a mythical tale that Bonnie had read a while ago, the young woman did not dare to look back, fearful of what she might see. Yet, what lay ahead of her was, perhaps, even more frightening.

At the door to the workshop, Bonnie waited for a reprimand that did not come. Part of her wanted her mother to stop her, wanted an explanation, wanted to be assured that what she suspected about her father was nothing more than wild imagination, but there was only silence and the faint scream of hinges as she stepped into the workshop once more.

Her father sat where she had left him, sweat glistening upon his brow, perspiring under the heat of at least fifteen candles and lanterns that were arranged in a horseshoe around him.

A bucket of sand occupied its own stool, within easy reach if sparks should fly and a fire should spread.

"Who goes there?" Bernard's eyes turned in his daughter's direction, and she prayed it was only the darkness beyond his ring of light that delayed his recognition of her.

"Bonnie wanted to see if you'd eaten your cake," Clara replied, resting a hand upon Bonnie's shoulder. "I told her to leave you be, but she insisted."

Bernard squinted, rubbing eyes that were already dappled with rough patches of red. Friction burns. "I didn't have much of an appetite, lass," he told his daughter with a smile so sad that it splintered Bonnie's heart. "But I'll have it for my breakfast."

On the workbench, piles of garnet silk were strewn in every direction, and Bernard's fingers were wrapped in thin bandages. For a man who relied upon a delicate touch for his craftsmanship, those bandages must have been a curse, making his needlework clumsy.

"What are you not saying?" Bonnie could hold her tongue no longer. "I am six-and-ten, not four-years-old. I am not a dolt. I know you are both hiding something from me, and... I would hear it from you instead of making my own guesses."

Her mother and father exchanged a look... or tried to. Her father squinted at the spot where he must have thought his wife was standing, but he was, in fact, staring at a supporting wooden pillar. Perhaps, Bonnie could have ignored that, but she could not ignore the pink hue, shot through with threads of livid red, that coloured the whites of his eyes. Nor could she neglect to see the crusts of dried-up secretions that clung to his lashes and gathered in the corners of those corrupted eyes.

"Are you unwell?" Bonnie pressed when she received no answer from her parents. "Shall I send for a doctor?"

Her father sighed and shook his head, setting down a scalloped sleeve that, even at a distance, appeared crooked. "The doctor has been, several times. There's nothing he can do for me." His brow creased as he glanced down at his hands, bringing them up to his face until his palms were almost touching his cheeks. "I thought it would pass—the doctor said it might—but it has not. And you are quite right; I shouldn't hide this from you any longer, though I must urge you not to say anything to Alice."

"I won't breathe a word," Bonnie promised, wringing her hands.

"I am losing my sight, dearest Bonnie," her father began in a heavy voice. "This past week, it has been fading more quickly than before. I... thought I had longer, but... my sight is almost gone." His breath caught as he spoke, hitching every few words as if it was a terrible struggle to admit the truth. "I can see shapes, I can see light and shadow, I can see everything in a blur, but the details of things—it is impossible. I can't do... I can't..."

Even though she had seen her father weep, it was the first time she had seen him break. It was akin to watching a person collapse in on themselves, the essence of who they were crumbling to dust, leaving a husk behind. Her father did not even cry, this time; he simply stared blankly down at the cresting waves of red silk that he could not see properly, his body trembling as if the cold of outside had snuck in through the cracks in the windows and in his very soul.

Bonnie rallied, swallowing down her own despair as she went to her father. "What can I do? My stitching has vastly improved, and I've watched you enough times to be of help. Tell me, Papa, what do you need? I won't sleep until it's done, and after that... well, we don't need to think about that, right now. Let's concentrate on just this one gown."

"It's too much," her father replied, shaking his head. "It can't be done."

"It can and it will," Bonnie insisted, removing the sand bucket from the nearby stool and taking her place at her father's side. "So, instruct me."

Across the workshop, Bonnie's mother observed the scene with shining eyes. She sniffed and turned her face away, discretely brushing something from her cheek as she strove to steady her breaths.

How long have you known, Mama? Bonnie wondered. *How long have you carried the burden of worry by yourself?* She thought of the cake and her stomach sank, for that confection might have been more costly than she realised: a luxury that they could not afford, if her father could no longer work.

"The inlay needs to be sewn into place," her father began hesitantly, moving his stool along the bench so Bonnie could sit in front of the fabrics. "That black material, there. And when that is done, everything needs to be sewn together. The entire gown. I... I'm sorry, Bonnie."

Bonnie put on her best smile. "Don't apologise, Papa. Just teach me. Pretend I'm William." She hesitated. "Shouldn't we send for him? Two pairs of hands might work swifter than one."

"No," her father replied sternly. "William is not to know."

"As you like." Bonnie would not argue. She had no time to.

Remembering her vow to make something of herself, she took up the already-threaded needle and set to work, guiding the sharp point through the fragile silk and pulling it through, before repeating the process over and over. It was painstaking, and it was immediately obvious that she lacked the level of talent that her father possessed, but nothing could be done about that now. Perhaps, by the end of the gown, her stitching would be almost as neat.

As long as the customer has a completed garment by tomorrow morning, all will be well. We will think of something. We will find a way to push through this, like a needle tugged through old leather, she told herself as she worked, for if she considered the alternative, her hands would shake, and this gown would never be finished. It would be suitable only for the ash pile.

***

By dawn, all hope had been unpicked from the shining gown, all prospects for the future left in tatters. The inlay had been sewn into place, but there was no possible way for the rest of the dress to be completed in time for the express rider that would come to the shop at nine o'clock. Bonnie's fingers ached, her back spasmed, her shoulders were knotted stiff, and her neck felt like it had forgotten how to hold up the weight of her head. And whilst she had a new admiration for her father's toil, layered upon the absolute respect she already possessed, that would not serve them in getting the gown done.

"It is finished," her father said softly, as the first glimpse of daylight—ashy and blue—filtered in through the small, oval window that offered a view into the shop beyond.

"Not yet, Papa, but I will keep going," Bonnie promised.

Her father managed a tight laugh. "That's not what I meant, darling. I meant, it's finished—I'm finished." An odd sound, partway between a sob and a yelp, came strangled out of his throat. "Making beautiful gowns and finely tailored garments is all I've ever known. It has given us a fine life, a life I could never imagine for myself when I was a younger man, but... it is done. If I cannot continue, then..." He faltered, as if it was not only the words he was struggling to form, but a vision of the future, too.

What will happen to us? Bonnie did not dare to ask. But there was one thing she *did* dare to ask—a demand that could no longer be avoided.

"Let me fetch William," she urged. "I would need a week to finish this, but William can do it quicker. Quick enough to keep this customer happy, at least. After that, perhaps he can make all the gowns and do all the tailoring under your observation. You can instruct, he can make, and everything might be all right."

Her father shook his head slowly, his eyes pinched as if he had already contemplated the notion. "William has stiff technique and lacks creativity and inspiration. He will not be able to fulfil our orders, even with my tutelage."

Bonnie found that very hard to believe, for she had enjoyed countless conversations in this very workshop with William, poring over his secret book of illustrations and designs that he had not dared to show to her father.

William spoke of gowns and fine suits in the same way that her father did; his green eyes— the colour of summer ivy—shining with passion when he waxed poetic about sourcing new fabrics from the Orient: fabrics that would move like liquid when a lady danced or change colours depending on how the light hit it, and would make his work the talk of not just England but the Continent. How could her father think that William lacked inspiration? She thought about saying so, but the expression on her father's face warned her against it.

"Still, I think it prudent to fetch him," she said instead. "You say he lacks your gift, and perhaps you are right, but he has enough of a knack for sewing to get this gown completed before the lady it is intended for explodes in a rage."

Her father bowed his head and gave the smallest nod. "Very well, but you mustn't tell him why. Tell him... I have a sudden sickness, nothing more."

"Of course, Papa. I shan't be long." Bonnie slid off the stool, feeling every ache and knot that the night had twisted into her muscles and cracked deep into her bones.

Bolting out of the shop, she hitched up her skirts and ran faster than she had ever had a need to run before. Overhead, the orange and pink stains of dawn bled through dark rainclouds, urging her legs to move faster. To Bonnie, the threat of imminent daylight was a gigantic clock, clanging above her, thundering out every second until nine o'clock, when the express rider would come for the gown. It had to be finished. William could do it; she knew he could, for the entire future of her family hinged upon it.

But what if he can't? her mind whispered, turning her heart into an icy stone that sank down into her churning stomach. William would do his best, but what if his best simply was not good enough?

"We will be ruined," she gasped as her shoes pounded the pavement, beating out a death knell for life as she knew it.

Chapter Three

Thanks to William, crisis had been averted on that cold and rainy morning; his diligence and speed ensuring that the beautiful gown of garnet silk was placed, completed, into the hands of the express rider and carried away to the lady who would likely wear it only once. Bonnie had always thought that to be very wasteful indeed, but she could not complain when it kept food upon the table and coal in the fireplace.

There had been an article in the newspaper a few days after that hellish night and morning of unceasing toil, brimming with compliments for the daring gown and the young Countess who had worn it, but there had been no applauding or congratulating in the gloomy workshop of Acklam & Sons, where detailed orders and designs were stacked high on inky leaves of paper, and the entire place looked as if it was suffering the aftermath of a battle. Fabric exploded everywhere, spilling from the workbenches and cupboards and drawers in rainbow entrails. Sewing needles glinted menacingly on every surface and even on the sawdust-covered floor, whilst thimbles and spools of thread were discarded in violence, thrown hither and thither at each peak of Bernard Acklam's ongoing frustration.

"You can't curse your sight back," Bonnie had heard her mother whispering to her father the previous night, after he had torn up the beginnings of an exquisite skirt of cerulean blue. "Go to the Minster and pray, if it'll ease your restless spirit, but don't go hurlin' expensive fabrics across the room. That's not goin' to help no-one."

Bonnie had heard her father storm out of the shop after that, though she could only guess where he had marched away to. Worried, she had taken his place as she had done every night since learning of his blindness, looking over the designs for the next gown, and doing what she could to fix what he had torn with the help of the *Singer* sewing machine that had been sat in the corner gathering dust since her father had bought it a few years prior. He hated the thing and often threatened to sell it, but it could do the work much faster than Bonnie's unaccustomed fingers could. Every night, she grew more grateful that he had not followed through with his threat.

When her father had returned that morning, while she had been hard at work, relentlessly pressing the wrought iron foot pedal and pulling the delicate fabric through the needle mechanism, her father had reeked of potent liquor. His eyes had been cobwebbed with tiny threads of garnet red, his nose almost purple, his gait unsteady as he had bumped and swayed his way through the shop and into the workshop. Bonnie had intervened before he could cause too much damage, grabbing him by the arm and steering him back out into the hallway, where she had helped him up the stairs to the apartments above.

It had been hours since that unsettling entrance, and though Bonnie had distracted herself with soothing the temperamental moods of the *Singer*, she kept listening for sounds of life: her father's familiar footfalls on the stairs; his cheerful morning humming; the whistle of the kettle on the stove. Anything to let her know that the previous night had been a unique incident, never to be repeated.

As for Bonnie's mother, Clara; she had taken charge of her husband after Bonnie had managed to get him up the stairs and, after urging him into the bedchamber, Clara had re-emerged to prepare two thick slices of bread and a chunk of crumbly white cheese, accompanied by a pitcher of weak ale. Bonnie had looked on, waiting for her mother to tell her that everything would be well, whilst drunken snores had rumbled out of the bedchamber door.

"I've never known Papa to drink," Bonnie had said, at last: the silence unbearable.

Her mother had shrugged. "Sometimes, there's nothin' else a man can do."

"Won't it harm his eyes? They looked... all red."

Her mother had paused in preparing the food, standing with her back to Bonnie. The older woman's shoulders had sagged, and a long, weary sigh had whispered from tired lungs, slumping her shoulders even further, until it looked like Clara Acklam had withdrawn into herself. "It hardly matters now," was all she had said, before she had taken the bread and cheese and pitcher into the bedchamber and left Bonnie alone in the kitchen.

Somehow, that had troubled Bonnie more than if her mother had dragged her father out into the street to shout and scream and slap some sense into him, as Bonnie had witnessed other wives doing with their inebriate husbands. Instead, her mother's resignation sent a chill down her spine, like her mother knew this was just how things were going to be from now on. And that was like a fishbone in Bonnie's throat— hard to swallow.

Yet, Bonnie could not rest on her laurels. *Someone* had to make sure the orders were completed, and if that someone had to be her, then so be it. And she figured there was no better practice than the panicked act of getting everything completed as swiftly as possible. Even when she was not fulfilling orders, she was practicing on spare scraps of fabric to improve her stitching. After all, it could not all fall to William, who had a sickly mother to take care of. He came by at nine o'clock every morning to begin his daily work and left at six o'clock in the evening, and she refused to ask anything more of him.

So, it came as something of a surprise when the back door of the workshop creaked open, and a figure stole in on furtive footsteps. It was not yet six o'clock in the morning, the winter darkness still unbroken by the dawn light. In the workshop, with only two lanterns to see by, Bonnie feared the worst: a thief, come to steal as many valuable bolts of silk as possible. It would not have been the first time that the shop had been attacked.

Picking up a sharp pair of fabric scissors, she jumped up from her spot by the sewing machine and wielded them at the intruder, shaking from head to toe at the unexpected interruption.

"Announce yourself!" she hissed, swallowing thickly.

A gasp soughed through the gloom and the figure halted sharply, putting up two hands of eager surrender. "It's me," the voice said quietly.

The voice was blissfully familiar, though Bonnie did not immediately set down the scissors. "William?"

"I've got to say, I wasn't expecting such an... aggressive welcome," he replied, with a nervous chuckle in his voice. "Yes, it's me."

"Why would you come in through the back door?" Bonnie put the scissors down and lifted a lantern, casting the hazy glow onto her father's apprentice.

William flashed a grin. "I wasn't expecting anyone else to be down here, and I thought I'd wake everyone if I came in through the front. That bell over the door is louder than you think."

He was as handsome as ever, with a mane of golden-brown hair that he often held back, out of his face, with a black ribbon when he was working. Bonnie often though he resembled a lion, with his wide, almost feline nose, and his freckled complexion that browned in the summer, but he had the gentleness of a house cat. His almond-shaped, green eyes were still wide in residual fright as he stared back at her; his large, rough hands still up in surrender.

Bonnie had known him since he was a boy, the two of them often getting into trouble as they ran wild through the streets of York, but as they had grown beyond childhood, that mischief had no longer seemed appropriate. Indeed, at seven-and-ten, William had become quite the young gentleman: tall and broad-shouldered, always well-dressed in the attire that her father had given him, cutting a fine figure wherever he went—a walking ambassador for the shop's sartorial delights. And with his warm eyes and kindly demeanour, he had no shortage of young ladies enquiring after him. But his work and his apprenticeship and his poorly mother always came first. Sometimes, Bonnie was not even sure if William knew he had transformed into such a desirable prospect, for he treated everyone with the same gentility and never showed any awareness when a young lady attempted to flirt with him.

"It's not yet nine," Bonnie pointed out.

"I thought I'd come early to start on... well, that." He nodded toward the cerulean blue gown that cascaded from the *Singer's* jaws. "I could begin with Lord Redmond's tailcoat, if you have the gown in hand?"

Bonnie paused. "I'm agreeable to that. I'm getting better with the gowns, but I can't stand all the finicky sewing with the gentlemen's attire. You'd assume it'd be the other way around."

"Just wait until we start on the beading for Lady Croft's gown." William shuddered and, for the first time in several days, Bonnie allowed herself to laugh. William not only had a knack for tailoring and sewing; he had a knack for putting her at ease, too. Whenever he was around her, nothing seemed as bad. At the very least, she could forget how bad things were for a short while.

"Are you hungry?" she asked.

He patted his stomach. "Famished."

"I'll fetch us something whilst you settle yourself."

With that, Bonnie slipped out of the workshop and crept up the stairs to the apartments above. No one stirred from either of the occupied bedchambers and the kitchen hearth lay cold and dead, though there was plenty of shiny, black coal in the scuttle beside the fireplace. There was nothing waiting on the stove to be warmed up for breakfast either, though Bonnie managed to pilfer a few cold cuts of ham, some cheese, and an apple.

She buttered a slice of bread to accompany the rest of the meagre meal, feeling guilty with every swipe of the knife across the crumbed square. Perhaps, her mother had been saving the delicacies, but if Bonnie and William were to endure another lengthy day of sewing, they would need sustenance.

"Forgive me, Mama," Bonnie murmured, for though they had yet to fail in fulfilling an order, she sensed that the sleepless nights and relentless days would soon become unfeasible. Already, Bonnie was beginning to feel the effects, and dazed concentration was not conducive to well-made gowns.

Returning to the workshop, Bonnie portioned up the breakfast goods and sat down at the workbench to share the meal with William. Despite the hectic nature of the work they had to complete, both seemed content to take a moment to simply enjoy hearty food and conversation before the hours of sewing rendered them silent and solitary.

"How is your father faring today? Will he be joining us for the day's thrilling exploits?" William bit off a piece of bread, grinning as he chewed.

Bonnie wished she could smile along with him. "He was... um... sewing until an ungodly hour again, so I imagine he'll be resting until past noon. Perhaps later."

"Past noon?" William arched an eyebrow. "How very specific of you. If I didn't know any better, I'd say he'd had himself a drink and might be nursing a sore head."

"Then, it's lucky you *do* know better," Bonnie retorted, her face flushing with uncomfortable heat. "My father doesn't drink."

William chewed another mouthful of bread and ham; his expression thoughtful. "Is he still feeling unwell? If he is, he shouldn't be toiling away in the workshop until he's improved. The light and heat of this room is enough to make anyone feel worse when they're already poorly. I remember suffering last year with a terrible winter cold, and I was convinced I was dying until your father told me to step outside and draw in some fresh air. The difference was staggering."

"It does seem to be a... uh... lingering sort of sickness. One of those same winter colds that clings on for weeks," Bonnie replied, feeling a little guilty. She hated lying to her oldest friend, especially when she did not truly understand why she had to lie to him.

What harm could it do if William knew what was wrong with her father? He was not the sort of man who would shirk his duties. Indeed, she was certain he would leap at the chance to repay her father for his kindness over the years, for her father was the one who had paid for William's mother's medicines and doctors. Yet, Bonnie's father continued to insist that William could not know of the degenerative blindness that would eventually leave Bernard Acklam entirely unable to perform his lifelong work.

Pride, I imagine, Bonnie had concluded, though she had never thought of her father as a proud man.

"I know all about those," William replied with a fond, sad smile. "My own ma has had a lingering winter cold for... oh, years now."

"How is she faring?" Bonnie thought it only polite to ask.

William sighed and bent to pick up all of the sewing needles that had been abruptly discarded. If he thought there was something strange about the strewn needles and thimbles and fabrics and tools, he did not say so.

Then again, it had become something of a ritual in the week since the red gown had been completed: William came into the shop, witnessed the destruction, and set about picking everything up and restoring the workshop to some semblance of its former neatness. Bonnie suspected he knew more of the truth than he was letting on, but she admired him for not prying further.

"She's no better, no worse," William said, sticking the needles back into a stuffed, knitted wool ball, shaped like an apple. Bonnie's mother had made it for Bernard when they first married, and the famed dressmaker and tailor had cherished it ever since.

That done, William returned his attention to the slices of real apple that sat on a plate, waiting to be devoured. He passed a slice to Bonnie, and they ate in contemplative silence, both mulling over the woes of their respective parents.

"You'd tell me if there was something more… concerning afoot with your father, wouldn't you?" he asked, all of a sudden. "I know it's not my place to speak of it, but when your father has been unwell before, he has never requested that you become his substitute. Yet, every morning when I have arrived, you have been hunched over that sewing contraption, resembling a husk with each passing day. I have begun to wonder if you are sleeping at all, in truth, and if you are not sleeping—my question, I suppose, is why?"

Bonnie cursed inwardly, aware that William was no fool who could be easily hoodwinked. Whilst she had always shown a keen interest in her father's work, forever finding excuses to loiter in the workshop as her father and William discussed the day's creations, she had never made a full gown before necessity had demanded it, nor had she shown any indication that she wished to make dressmaking her vocation.

Indeed, a young woman of her station was not expected to have any vocation at all, other than the pursuit of becoming a wife and mother.

"It is necessary," was all Bonnie could say, refusing to look her dear friend in the eyes. "He is aware of your additional duties, beyond this workshop, and he doesn't wish to burden you."

"Burden me? Now, I'm certain there's something afoot here." William narrowed his eyes. "For months, I have asked your father if I might work longer hours, so I hardly think he would consider it burdensome."

Bonnie nearly choked on the bread she was eating. "Perhaps, the fever made him forget that you'd asked. Either way, this is what he wants, and I won't argue with his instructions."

"I will," William shot back, shaking his head. "It's unseemly for a young lady like yourself to be labouring away like one of the lasses who work at the seam. If you didn't have two ha'pennies to rub together, maybe I'd be less suspicious, but your father's gowns continue to be the talk of England. So, what is the matter? What aren't you saying? I thought we trusted one another."

"I do trust you," Bonnie began to insist, "but—" Her words were strangled into a gasp of terror as an almighty scream ripped through the workshop, splintering down the stairs and through the door from the apartments above.

Without thinking, she shot across the workshop and up the stairs, following the blood-curdling sound all the way to her parents' bedchamber. There, she skidded to a halt in the open doorway, panting as if she had sprinted a marathon. Her hands braced against her sides, her chest heaving against the boning of her corset, straining for greater freedom as her eyes peered helplessly into the anaemic glow of the room beyond.

There, upon the bed, her father sat bolt upright in his wife's arms, wailing like a wounded animal as his beloved held him close and sobbed into his shoulder. Both were shaking violently, both seized in the grip of unbearable agony, both lost in one another's grief, unaware of their eldest daughter standing on the threshold of the room, frozen in fear.

"What's the matter?" Bonnie managed to rasp, her heart in her throat. "What has happened?"

Her father raised his head, gazing toward the sound of her voice, but his streaming eyes were unfocused, looking past her as his strained expression twisted into a mask of chilling panic. "I... can't see," he wheezed, as if admitting it stole every scrap of air from his lungs. "I can't see anything at all. I am... blind, Bonnie. I am... blind."

A floorboard creaked behind her, a second set of panting breaths matching her own. She did not need to turn to know who it was; William had followed her up the stairs, and he had heard everything. The truth, harrowing as it was, could not be hidden any longer.

Chapter Four

For a fortnight, the fates conspired in myriad ways to help and hinder the struggling souls who sweated and bled and ached through every stitch of the gowns and garments that somehow staggered out of the closed doors of Acklam & Sons. Each day, small crowds of puzzled customers gathered on the icy street, peering in through the dusty windows, harassing the door handle as if that might encourage the shop to open once more.

"I hear they are only taking commissions," one young lady had remarked in a hushed tone.

"Well, I hear they have a horde of children in the basement, sewing ceaselessly," another commented, most unkindly.

"Whatever the matter is, I do hope they open again soon," a third had mumbled, blowing warm breath into her gloved hands. "I am to be married soon, and I have dreamed of walking towards my love in a gown from Acklam & Sons."

Meanwhile, Bonnie and William felt no relief at the shop's temporary closure, for they had more orders than anyone could possibly complete alone, and the longer it took them to finish one tea dress or ball gown or tailcoat, the less time they had for the next order. It was akin to trying to outpace a flood, and both were floundering for some hint of high ground.

"You've toiled away in here for almost three years with my father," Bonnie said, stretching out her stiff back. "How does he do it? How could he possibly manage all of this by himself? He has always told us that he only takes the commissions he can complete to the finest quality, and yet... this seems never-ending."

William dragged his shirt sleeve across his glistening brow. "I couldn't tell you, but I've seen him complete two gowns in one day, without a single stitch gone awry. I've seen him conjure a pile of dinner jackets and opera cloaks in an afternoon, and never thought to question the magic of it. He must be a sorcerer; it's the only explanation." He puffed a breath upward, blowing a lock of golden-brown hair out of his face. "Now, if he'd just tell us which devil he sold his soul to, I'll arrange an appointment immediately."

Bonnie mustered a feeble smile. "I'm pleased it's not just me that thinks this is… ludicrous. I thought you might have scolded me by now for falling behind."

"Why would I scold you? At times, I swear you are ahead of me, though *I* do not have that unholy contraption at my disposal." He chuckled but it did not reach his tired green eyes. "Are you sleeping, Bonnie? I mean no insult, but you do not look well, and if you continue in this manner, I shall have to accept defeat for I can't do this alone."

"Ah, and there I was, thinking you were actually concerned for my welfare," Bonnie teased, blushing a little.

"I am, but I also have wholly selfish reasons for asking," he quipped in reply, dragging his stool over to where she sat in the corner, poised in front of the *Singer.*

She cut a loose thread with the fabric scissors and slid the silky material out of the stabbing stinger of the needle mechanism, admiring her improving handiwork. "I am sleeping enough," she told him, pursing her lips as she noticed a crooked seam. "Mama makes certain that I do."

"And do you stay in your chambers, or do you sneak back out to work some more?" William cast her a knowing glance, as she settled into the tedious task of unpicking everything she had spent the past half an hour on perfecting.

"I won't see Alice starve," Bonnie muttered, praying the fragile silk would not fray as the threads were cut free. "Mama has to tend to Papa, so if I must toil with all my might until these last orders are complete, then I shall endure to the bitter end."

William expelled a deep sigh. "Does Alice know?"

"She suspects something is amiss, but we have explained that Papa is merely unwell; she lacks the details, and I hope to keep it that way."

"Until when?"

Bonnie glanced at him in confusion. "Pardon?"

"Until when?" he repeated, resting a gentle hand upon her forearm. "After these orders are completed, what then? Will you continue to replace your father, hiding the truth from everyone? Will we continue like this, breaking our backs to avoid discovery?"

It was a conundrum that Bonnie had considered at least hourly for the past two weeks, and yet no clear answer would come to her.

"We shall take more commissions. *Fewer* commissions. Enough to manage, but not too few that we'll lose all we have," she replied, with more confidence than she felt. "Unless, you are contemplating abandoning us?"

William smiled. "I couldn't abandon you, even if you forced me out of the door with your own bare hands. You're as much my family as my own flesh and blood." He nudged her in the arm. "And I remember how you used to box my ears when I was a lad. I wouldn't risk facing that again, now you're fully grown."

His words soothed her like salve on a skinned knee, cooling the sting of her fears for the future. As long as she had him at her side, she knew things could never become intolerable.

Indeed, throughout the past fortnight, she had come to rely upon him in a way she had never expected, their friendship transforming into something altogether more precious.

His was the face she looked forward to seeing in the morning, her eyes peering over at the clock on the mantelpiece as she counted the minutes until his arrival, when he would fill the silence and make the cold workshop seem that little bit warmer.

His was the voice she longed to hear, even if they spoke of nothing but the weather. His was the presence she wished to be near to, for her very soul believed that he was the only one who could protect her and her family now.

"I'm glad of that," she said softly. Shyly.

His gaze drifted toward the small window in the back door, that looked out onto the grim alley behind the shop.

His eyebrows raised in surprise, prompting Bonnie to follow his line of sight.

"It's snowing," William gasped. "I thought the sky looked peculiar on my way here."

Bonnie's heart swelled, for she had always adored the snow. She could vividly remember one winter when she was younger, when she had played in the thick snow drifts for hours with William; the two of them borrowing a neighbour's sledge to take to one of nearby slopes that angled sharply down from the ancient city walls.

The walk back up to the top after sliding down had thawed the frost in her bones, her legs aching by the time she was called in for supper by her mother. She remembered falling asleep by the fire, curled up like a kitten, content in a way she had not been since.

How blissful it is to be a child, she mused sadly, as fluffy snowflakes floated down, muffling the city in an eerie silence as bruised clouds, the colour of photographs, prepared to blanket the cobbled streets and bygone strongholds.

***

By evening, the slow snowfall had warped into a blizzard, battering the city and every remnant of its rich history with howling winds and snowflakes that whipped the skin like tiny shards of broken glass.

The snow lay thick on the ground outside, banking against doors and windows, freezing locks and breathing ghostly cobwebs onto the glass panes that could do nothing to prevent the shrieking gales from whistling in.

In the workshop, Bonnie and William huddled by the fireplace, rationing out the coal that remained in the scuttle. The Acklam family were not yet impoverished, the steady stream of income from the gowns and tailoring still flowing into the coffers, but it was as if they were bracing for a proverbial rainy day.

Still, sewing so many garments was difficult enough when Bonnie and William had full dexterity in their fingers, and the cold would soon render it impossible to proceed if they did not purchase more of that black gold. It was an expense that could not be spared.

"I'll venture out and fetch us some more," William announced, his teeth chattering as he moved to collect his great coat from the hook on the wall. "I have coin enough, and John Deeks sells it cheap. Moreover, he owes me a favour."

Bonnie thought about arguing, but her limbs and lips were too numb to conjure a protest. "Take my... father's scarf," she urged, hugging herself as she stared into the fireplace and watched the dimming embers as the coal collapsed into ash. Even with the help of the *Singer*, her footwork upon the pedal had become sloppy; each shake and tremble of her legs speeding up the mechanism when she meant to slow it down. If she could not warm herself, it would take twice as long to complete the burnished orange gown that was due for collection the following morning.

Perhaps, the snow will prevent the rider from coming. Perhaps, this is the heavens granting us a strange sort of reprieve, she hoped desperately, offering a weak wave to William as he hurried out into the bitter storm. The door screamed in complaint, a mighty gust of icy wind whirling all the way through to the workshop, before William managed to battle the door back into the jamb.

Bonnie raced to the small, oval window that looked out into the shop, standing on tiptoe so she could see the front windows and the street beyond. William walked by, braced against the inclement weather, bent almost diagonal as he pushed through the gales on his quest for coal.

Just then, light footsteps drew Bonnie's attention toward the door to her right. Someone was coming downstairs, treading carefully as if they meant to sneak up on her.

The door opened and Alice stepped in, rubbing bleary eyes. "Did someone go out?" she asked, stifling a yawn.

"William," Bonnie replied, beckoning for her little sister to come to her. "Have you been sleeping?"

Alice nodded and walked into her sister's arms, hugging her tightly. "I don't feel very well. It's too cold upstairs and Mama says we can't have a fire." She paused, peering up at Bonnie. "Why can't we have a fire, Bonnie? Mama won't tell me, and Papa won't leave his bed. Is he terribly sick? I... tried to bring him some tea, but... he shouted at me to get out. I... don't know what... I did wrong."

Bonnie gripped her sister with all of her might, pressing a reassuring kiss to the little girl's soft, shiny hair. "You did nothing wrong, sweetpea. No one has done anything wrong. Papa is... very poorly, but all will be well. William and I will make sure of it, and Mama will soon have a fire roaring in the grate upstairs again, and you won't be so cold anymore."

"Is Papa going to... die?" Alice hiccoughed, burying her face in Bonnie's shoulder.

Bonnie squeezed her eyes shut, wishing they could all return to the morning of her birthday, when everything was well and no dark clouds threatened their happiness. She wished they could return to when they were lucky and grateful for their good fortune, when her back and shoulders and hands did not ache and twinge with every waking and slumbering moment. Selfishly, she wished she had never been made to glimpse a different life, where hard work would be demanded of her. Perhaps, she *had* taken the life they used to have for granted, believing they would always be comfortable and well-off.

"Papa will recover," she said, though she could not promise it. According to the physician who had been and gone twice in the past fortnight, there was nothing else amiss with her father's health, but as he would not eat, could not sleep, and was slowly being driven toward a terrifying kind of madness by the loss of his greatest passion, Bonnie knew that his otherwise rude health might soon fail.

Alice clung to Bonnie. "Do you swear it?"

"I do," Bonnie lied, for what else could she do?

"Are you going to marry William?" Alice's voice softened to a curious shade of shy. "Is he going to own the shop while papa is sick?"

Bonnie's eyes widened in surprise. "Marry William? Whatever made you say that?"

"You're six-and-ten. Lots of girls get married at six-and-ten, and William likes you. Why wouldn't you get married?" Alice replied, with a strange wisdom beyond her young years. "Better than marrying a gentleman you don't like, or who doesn't like you."

At that moment, the front door blasted open, gusting William in as if cued. He carried a large parcel under one arm and had a newspaper over his face, likely to stave off the worst of the stinging snow. Cheeks nipped red by the cold, blowing into his hands as he set the newspaper down on the workbench, he immediately joined the sisterly huddle, wrapping his arms around Bonnie and Alice both.

"Let me steal a smidgen of your heat, eh?" he said, chuckling.

Bonnie froze in his embrace, uncertain of herself. Her stomach fluttered traitorously, her heart racing at the touch of his hand upon her sore back, her cheeks flooding with heat until they were likely the same colour as his. All because of her little sister's not-so-subtle suggestion that the man Bonnie had spent a fortnight working alongside might become a more permanent fixture in her life, if she would just pursue it.

William? He would not be such a terrible prospect, she considered, as he drew her warmth from her body, into his own. She did not mind sharing, not with him. After all, for two weeks, they had shared everything else: meals, conversation, duties, and she had even fallen asleep upon his shoulder once, when the hour had grown late, and the day's efforts had got the better of her.

"Have you come to join our merry band of needleworkers?" William asked, pulling away. He moved to the fireplace and crouched low, depositing his parcel full of coal into the scuttle.

Alice pulled a face. "Certainly not. I would die of boredom."

"Alice," Bonnie chided. "There are far worse things in this world than honest work. You would do well to remember that."

Alice's sour expression transformed into something akin to worry. "But *I* won't have to work, will I?"

Bonnie was saved from replying by her mother's voice, shouting down the stairs for her youngest daughter. "Alice, come here and help me stuff the cracks in the windows!"

"You'd best hurry before we all catch a chill," Bonnie said softly, ushering her sister toward the staircase.

Once Alice was safely upstairs, Bonnie paused beside the workbench, bracing her hands against the worn surface as she fought to steady her breathing. It was like a sickness, in and of itself, not to know what the future held. The stress of uncertainty kept her awake at night, even though she barely slept, and would have robbed her of her appetite, leaving her in the same condition as her father, if her mother and William did not ensure that she ate.

"It will not come to that," William said, appearing at Bonnie's side. He rested his hand between her shoulder blades, rubbing slow, small circles of reassurance. "She won't ever have to suffer."

Bonnie swallowed thickly. "How can you be sure?"

"I told you before; I won't let it happen. I won't let this shop or your father's lifelong work crumble away to ash," he promised. "Even if it is never my name above the lintel, I won't mind as long as I can keep you all safe. It is the least I can do, considering all that you have done for me. Your father, in particular. I doubt my mother would be alive if it were not for his generosity, and I might have starved when I was a child if you had not fed me from your own lunch pail."

Bonnie smiled in remembrance. "You were always ravenous."

"But I never went hungry, because of you," he replied, his eyes shining as they met hers.

The air between them crackled like the wide open moors before a summer thunderstorm, promising rain to slake the thirst of parched earth. A strange lump lodged in Bonnie's throat as she peered up at William, as though she was seeing him for the first time. Or seeing him with fresh eyes, at least. So many of her greatest memories had him at her side, their lives so intertwined that no amount of unpicking could unravel the entangled threads, but could Alice truly be right—did he like her beyond the boundaries of friendship?

Just then, Bonnie caught sight of something sticking out of William's lapels; a corner of paper, tucked into his waistcoat. One word was just visible: *Tattler.*

Without thinking, she reached for the corner of paper and pulled it free of William's waistcoat.

He tried to grasp for it, but that only made her more determined to possess it, stealing it away to the other side of the workbench where he would not be able to snatch it back.

"I didn't think you were an avid reader of the scandal sheets, William," she teased, but the look upon William's face—an expression of cold, dark dread—twisted her humour into a roiling unease.

"Please, return it to me. You should not see it," he begged, crestfallen.

She glanced down at the front page. "Whyever not? Are you in its wicked pages?"

"No, but it is not for your eyes." He tried to stretch across the workbench to seize it from her, but she turned her back, determined to investigate what she should not see.

The front page declared, in large letters: *Countess exposed at Winter Ball!*

That did not seem so unusual to Bonnie, for though she loathed the scandal sheets and everything they represented, its sole purpose was to humiliate the peerage. Yet, as she read on, she began to understand why William had done his best to hide it from her.

Wearing a daring gown of emerald green, procured from the famed dressmaker of River Row, Acklam & Sons, the young Countess was already the talk of Yorkshire before the mishap took place. In the midst of dancing with her husband, the Earl of Ripon, the grand gown seemed to rip of its own accord, the seams splitting and tearing until she resembled a scarlet woman on a Leeds street corner. Exposed and mortified, the poor Countess tried to flee, but tripped upon the torn garment, leaving nothing to the imagination of all those who were witness to the event.

It is not the first time that a gown from Acklam & Sons has incited public outrage, for not two weeks ago, the "Red Countess" also suffered embarrassment as her skirts tore away from her bodice. It was hastily pinned, of course, but one would expect better from a famed dressmaker. Perhaps, at last, old Bernard Acklam has lost his gift.

Bonnie's stomach lurched at the sight of her father's name being dragged through the ink, knowing that she was at fault. *She* was the one who had made the emerald gown, and she was the one who had tried to finish the red gown in haste.

"I have ruined him," she gasped, her voice shaky. "I have... ruined all of us."

William hurried to her side, putting a comforting arm around her. "It is one dress, Bonnie. Two, if you count the red one, but no one mentioned any mishap after the ball itself— indeed, this "Red Countess" was applauded for the beauty of the gown. Nothing will come of this, dear Bonnie. I promise, all will be well. Besides, no one who purchases their garments from here is likely to read such nonsense, and even if they do, they will know it is a young lady attempting to shroud her embarrassment in blaming someone else. Her husband must have stepped upon the skirts—everyone will know that."

But Bonnie knew better. Words had power in society, and gossip spread like wildfire through a gunpowder warehouse. This article *would* send her father's reputation up in smoke; it was just a matter of how quickly.

Still, as she took the scandal sheets to the fireplace and dropped them into the licking flames, she refused to believe it was all over. She *had* to salvage this, somehow, so her father would never have to know what she had done to ruin him and everything he had built over two decades in the span of a single fortnight.

Chapter Five

A week later, Bonnie learned how swift and devastating gossip could really be. The winter storm had subsided, and the dense snowdrifts had begun to melt, turning the streets into babbling streams, but neither the cold nor the damp could keep away the wolves that came to the door of Acklam & Sons, baying for blood.

"It was, of course, an unfortunate accident, but it cannot be blamed upon the craftsmanship of the garment itself," William tried to explain for the thousandth time that week, as another red-faced, angry customer stomped to the counter, demanding reimbursement for the order they had placed.

"The Countess's reputation will never recover, and I will *not* have my daughters embarrassed in the same fashion for wearing an unfit gown!" the customer—a portly, aggressive gentleman who reeked of brandy—replied, shaking his fists at William as Bonnie stood by, shamefaced.

"Consider all the other gowns that Bernard Acklam has crafted," William urged, as three more customers entered the shop. "Not one has torn or fallen to pieces. I do not wish to lay blame upon the poor lady, but the fault was not with our garments. Dresses do not rip at the seams without practical cause."

The unpleasant, purple-faced man leaned right over the counter and seized William by the lapels. "Now, listen here, you *will* reimburse me for the two gowns that have been ordered, and you will do so immediately, or I will seek recompense by taking my pound of flesh from you!"

The customers behind the fellow looked shocked by the outburst, but their horror soon transformed into agreement, as they began to call for their own compensation.

"The bodice of my daughter's gown has two tears in it already, and she received it not a month ago!" one woman declared.

"I have ordered a gown for my wedding, but I will not wear anything so shoddily crafted!" said another, as a meek gentleman at her side nodded feebly. Her future husband, no doubt.

Bonnie chewed the inside of her cheek, knowing that anger would not improve her situation. Yet, she could see these wretches for what they were—vultures, intent on trying to contrive a complimentary gown. Just two days ago, she had struggled to contend with a mother and daughter who had insisted that a gown and tea dress that they had purchased a year ago had been defective. In the end, Bonnie had threatened to summon the constables, calling them thieves, which had likely not helped her cause at all.

"If the gown you have ordered proves to be flawed when it is worn, then we shall, of course, reimburse you for the cost of it," William said firmly, undeterred by the fists gripping his lapels and pulling him half over the counter. "Until then, I would ask you to remove your hands from my tailcoat. If you cannot be civil, you won't speak to me at all."

The large man shoved William backwards, folding his arms across his barrel chest. "This will not be the last you hear from me. I will take receipt of the gowns that have been ordered, but if I find so much as a stitch out of place, I will return. And I shall *never* commission this wretched place again! You are not fit to sew my grandmother's drawers!"

He marched off without another word, slamming the shop door so hard that a crack appeared in one of the front windows. The other customers, having heard William's last remark, also decided to storm out of the shop, shouting at the tops of their lungs:

"We will have our coin returned!"

"We will bring you the evidence and then we shall see how proud you are!"

"This shop is a disgrace! You shall never see a single coin of mine again!"

Bonnie sagged onto a stool, holding her head in her hands as the last thud of the door in the jamb ricocheted through her skull.

She could already envision the endless stream of torn gowns and tea dresses and day dresses and tailcoats and waistcoats and trousers that would make their way into the shop in the coming days, ripped by the hands of those who thought they could recoup what they had spent by dastardly means.

"Lock the door," she pleaded, fighting back tears. "I can't bear to face another person today."

William sighed. "They are devils, every last one of them." He walked across the shop to the front door and opened it, peering out into the street. "And the most absurd part about it all is that the lady whose gown caused all of this has not come to seek compensation. She has likely given not a single thought to us or this shop or what her words might have done to us. There is no possibility in my mind that that gown tore of its own volition!"

"I never knew how awful people could be," Bonnie murmured, praying that her mother and father had not heard any of the ruckus. Fortunately, Alice was at the girls' grammar school that she attended each day, but Bonnie could only imagine what sort of torment her younger sister was facing from her peers. They would all know by now, gossiped at by their eager, conniving mothers.

"I shan't be a moment," William said suddenly, raising Bonnie's gaze to him as he stepped out into the street and closed the door gently behind him.

Curious, she slipped out from behind the counter and went to the water-stained window, peering left and right to see where he had gone. She spotted him a short distance down the street, greeting an older gentleman.

At first, Bonnie thought the fellow might be a customer, and William was trying to appease the man before he could even enter the shop, but as she continued to watch, the two gentlemen settled into what appeared to be a deep, amenable kind of discussion. There were smiles and laughter from both parties, and the older man clapped William on the back here and there, puzzling Bonnie. She had never seen the older man before, and there were not many acquaintances of William that she was not at least vaguely familiar with.

A few minutes later, after shaking hands, the two gentlemen parted ways. William returned to the shop, prompting Bonnie to run back behind the counter, so he would not know she had been watching.

As he locked the door, however, she could not help but ask, "Who were you speaking with out there?"

William kept his back turned. "No one. Just an acquaintance of my mother."

Perhaps, her nerves were already getting the better of her, considering the tirades she had endured that day, or perhaps it was the tone of William's voice—furtive and strange—but she was not certain she believed him. If the man was a friend of his mother's, why would William not invite him into the shop for some tea to warm himself?

"A close acquaintance?" she pressed, willing him to turn around.

When he did, however, she wished he had not. He wore a pinched expression, his gaze flitting anywhere but at her, his cheeks flushed pink though he had not been in the cold that long. In truth, he looked guilty, and she could not discern why.

"An old acquaintance," he replied, as he moved to take his greatcoat down from a nearby coat-stand. "Speaking of my mother, I said I would fetch her medicines for her, and as it seems we are to close the shop, I suppose now would be as good a moment as any. I'll return this evening to continue with our work."

Bonnie frowned. "You did not mention that before."

"In truth, I forgot." He flashed a grin that did not reach his eyes. "Evidently, I am a terrible son."

He made his way to the door that led into the workshop, skirting past her with the same guilty air as before. Bonnie followed, wishing he would put his arm around her again and put her at ease. Instead, he headed out of the back door, into the alley behind the shop, with a hurried wave and vanished from sight, leaving Bonnie wondering what on Earth had just happened, and *who* on Earth that strange older man might have been.

It is your mind, playing tricks, she told herself, retreating upstairs to the apartments. *You haven't slept, you haven't been eating properly, you have been fretting and worrying for weeks, and you have just listened to the atrocious things that people are saying, without due cause, about your father and his shop. Anyone would be teetering on a knife edge in such circumstances.* It did not soothe her to rationalise, but it served as a welcome distraction as she entered the kitchen, where her mother stood over the stove, absently stirring a pot that was on the brink of bubbling over.

Bonnie stepped in, taking the long, wooden spoon from her mother's hand and tending to the thin stew herself. It appeared they had begun to ration food as well as coal, suggesting that Bonnie's mother knew far more of what had been going on downstairs than she let on. Perhaps, she had always known it was inevitable.

"How is he?" Bonnie asked quietly as she stirred.

Her mother's mouth opened to answer, but a different sound splintered from the bedchamber, replying to Bonnie's question with a bestial wail and the jarring crash of something being thrown against a wall. The shattering noise was pursued by a frustrated bark that quickly descended into the babbling rant and rave of a lost soul who had released their grip upon sanity.

"Someone has done this!" her father howled. "Someone has taken my eyes from me! Someone has gouged them as I slept!" A second crash vibrated through the apartments, spearing the high-pitched crack of decimated ceramic into the kitchen, where it grated down each ridge of Bonnie's spine.

Her mother mustered a wan smile. "I suppose I don't need to answer that."

"No," Bonnie replied quietly, "I suppose not."

Whilst she had been fighting to save his life's work, exhausting herself at the *Singer* so she would not fall behind, her father had lost his mind. And as the physician had already informed the family that Bernard would never recover the loss of his sight, Bonnie realised that he would never recover the loss of his senses, either. Without purpose and passion, without fame and fortune, perhaps Bernard thought he no longer had anything to live for, forgetting the family who would have given their own sight if it could save him.

It is the end of us, Bonnie knew, feeling the rest of her fortitude trickling away with each sad belch of the bubbling, meagre stew.

Chapter Six

As winter closed in around the shop and the desolate family who clung to their existence within, the days so dark and the nights so long that Bonnie almost forgot what sunlight was, hopelessness knocked upon the door with the 'closed' sign upon it. Bonnie knew it was only a matter of time before she answered that knock and surrendered to whatever wretched creature had rapped its knuckles upon the wood.

Her father's condition continued to worsen, transforming him into a monster that she did not recognise. The humorous, generous, kindly man she adored and called "Papa" with a full and happy heart had been replaced with a twisted, cold changeling.

Now, her father spent his days in his bedchamber, refusing food, throwing it at the wall when it was brought to him, until rats began to creep into the apartments, eager for a taste of what had been discarded so violently.

Flies buzzed in the foetid realm that he had putrefied for himself, rejecting any request to bathe, denying Bonnie's mother's pleas to allow her to at least launder the blankets and coverlets that he wrapped himself in like a filthy cocoon.

Indeed, he only stirred to drink and rant, though Bonnie had no notion of where he was procuring the alcohol that he guzzled like a cure. She suspected her mother was bringing it to him as a means to soothe him in some small measure, and though she wished her mother would not do so, there was nothing she could do to stop it.

Her mother was suffering enough, relegated to sleeping on the floor in the kitchen, forbidden from getting too close to the man she had loved for twenty years. When she did get too close, he did not strike her, but his words were vile enough to be considered injurious.

All the while, Bonnie toiled at the *Singer* until she felt as if she had aged three decades in a matter of weeks. Her back now curved in a perpetual hunch, her fingers stiff and cold; her nails were tinged blue as the workshop fire continuously burned down to nothing. Her skin was dry and lined with hours upon hours of unbroken concentration, her lips cracked and bleeding, her stomach gnawing in complaint against the watery broths and stale bread and runny porridge that had become the family's only sustenance.

"Bonnie?" Her mother's voice drew her attention away from the rhythmic thudding of the needle mechanism and the whirr of her foot upon the pedal.

"Hmm?"

Her mother entered the workshop with a tray and came to perch on the low milking stool that William usually occupied when he wanted to be closer to the fire. Or Bonnie. "Have there been any more unwanted visitors today?" her mother asked, pushing a bowl of hot, thin soup into Bonnie's frozen hands.

"None," Bonnie replied stiffly, her jaw locked from shivering.

"That is… fortunate."

Bonnie took a tentative sip of the soup. It tasted of nothing but water and a hint of salt and the earthiness of carrot tops and turnip peelings and perhaps an old leaf of cabbage or two, judging by the flimsy, blanched fragments that floated in the broth. Still, it was warm, and her body awakened to the heat.

"It worries me," Bonnie admitted. "They all threatened to return, yet none of them have."

Her mother shrugged. "Let us consider it a mercy."

"In business, there is no mercy. Papa has always said that," Bonnie reminded her mother. "I can't fathom it, Mama. Where are they all? Why have they not come back with gowns they have torn with their own hands, demanding satisfaction? I do not wish it, do not mistake me, but it is preferable to this… unnerving quiet."

Her mother nudged the soup bowl, encouraging Bonnie to drink some more. "There have been letters for your father, but he has burned them before opening them."

"Then, why have you permitted him to have them?" Bonnie stared at her mother in disbelief. "He is not himself, Mama. There might be something in those letters that could explain the silence. What use is there in giving letters to a—" She halted sharply, unable to say the awful word that danced upon the tip of her tongue: lunatic.

"It isn't my place to read his letters, Bonnie," her mother replied evenly, though her eyes creased in doubt, as if questioning herself. "Has William not arrived yet?"

Bonnie thumbed at the back door. "He went to purchase coal. I asked him not to, but he wouldn't listen. I imagine the sound of my chattering teeth was becoming something of a distraction from his work." She meant it in jest, but as her mother's face fell, she wished she could take the remark back.

"Is there much to be done?" Her mother gestured at the bleak workshop: a shadow of its former glory. The cupboards looked as though they had been ransacked, half of the shelves bare of the bolts of vibrant fabric that her father would usually have delivered to the shop each month; sooner if an order called for something special. Yet, some valuable silks and satins and bombazines remained, and would fetch a fair price if it came to it.

Bonnie shook her head. "We are finishing the last two orders today. After that, there is nothing more to be done." Her words were more weighted than she had intended, but both mother and daughter seemed to feel the heaviness therein.

"Will the customers pay?" Her mother swallowed loudly.

"I can't know until delivery is made. Thus far, the majority have paid what is owed, but there is an... unscrupulous minority who are refusing. I doubt they will have any qualms about wearing the garments whilst spurning Papa's name in the same breath."

Her mother had found out about the article in the scandal sheets, and the bombardment of complaints that had pounded upon the shop door. Both women had decided, without discussion, to keep the truth from Bernard, though Bonnie doubted he would have heard anything they said, even if they had told him.

"Vermin," her mother spat, showing some emotion for the first time in a long while. "No, they are worse than vermin, for at least the rats are only trying to survive. Those scoundrels could pay for gowns and tea dresses ten times and still have plenty to spare."

Bonnie nodded. "I couldn't agree more." She paused, weary with the world. "I thought I might pay a visit to the mercer tomorrow, to sell what is left of Papa's fabrics."

"It has come to that?"

Bonnie drained what was left in the bowl, wiping her mouth on the back of her hand. "It has been weeks since there has been a new order. It is all we can do to keep afloat." She hesitated. "Does Alice suspect anything?"

"I fear so," her mother confessed. "The children at school have been sayin' cruel things. Just this mornin', she said she didn't want to go, but havin' her there is better than havin' her here, with her father rantin' and ravin' at every wakin' moment." Her rural accent strengthened with the grief that tightened around her throat; her eyes glistening with regret as she stared into the embers of the fireplace. "We'll have to set William loose."

"Pardon?" Bonnie sat up straighter in alarm.

"We can't afford to pay him," her mother replied plainly. "I'm certain he'll find employ elsewhere, but we have to take care of ourselves first. The money from these cloths and fabrics might stretch for another few months, and that's time we can't lose if we're to think of another way to manage."

Neither woman realised that the back door had opened, and William had entered, carrying a fresh parcel of coal for the scuttle. Only when he cleared his throat did Bonnie whirl around in fright, her heart sinking at the beautiful sight of him. He was her one joy, and if she lost him, she feared the darkness that paced around the perimeter of her mind might finally breach her walls and drag her down into despair.

He smiled at her, putting on a show of bravery. "I had a feeling this day would come, but there's no need to send me away, Mrs. Acklam. I'll finish what is left to be done, and I'll accompany Bonnie to the mercer tomorrow, and when that is done too, I'll... do all I can to help you." He set the coal down and shuffled off his greatcoat, as if he meant to stay for good. "If new orders should come in, I'll return and work without pay, for there's still a great deal that I owe Mr. Acklam."

"We couldn't ask that of you, William," Bonnie's mother insisted, but William waved away the protest.

"You don't have to ask. It's something I'd be honoured to do." His soft, reassuring gaze did not leave Bonnie's, making her wonder how she could ever have suspected him of some unknown guilt a week or so ago. William would never let her down; she knew that, deep in her heart.

Bonnie's mother looked like she might cry as she went to William and pressed a gentle kiss to his brow. "You are an angel in disguise, William Price." She held him for a while, and though he was too polite to embrace her in return, he rested his chin upon her shoulder and smiled over at Bonnie. "What would we do without you?"

"My chest will puff with so much pride that I won't be able to leave the shop if you keep complimenting me like that," William teased, as Bonnie's mother released him.

"Nonsense," the older woman scolded lightly. "You deserve congratulation for all you've done to help, these past weeks. They have been... very difficult, and I know that Bonnie has been grateful for your unyieldin' assistance."

William lowered his gaze, fidgeting as if the words made him shy. "I, too, have been grateful for Bonnie's fortitude. To my shame, I never knew she was as strong as she has shown herself to be. She continues to astonish me. Indeed, I..." He paused, like he meant to say something else, but his mouth closed and he returned to the fireplace, stoking the fire and leaving whatever he might have said unspoken.

"You what, William?" Bonnie pressed, her heart a caged bird in her chest, fluttering wildly.

"I am in awe of you," he replied, prodding the ashes, "that is all."

There was a thickness in his voice that suggested that was *not* all, but Bonnie was to bashful to investigate further, and too nervous that she might be mistaken. William was not a gentleman of means, necessarily, but he had a gift for the fashions of the day and his designs were almost as beautiful as Bernard's. As such, if William *were* to ask for her hand in marriage, perhaps it could be arranged for him to inherit the shop as a wedding gift and see Bonnie's father's legacy continued.

That would certainly help in skirting around the issue of the Countess's torn gown, and might draw customers back to the shop, if they learned it was under a new ownership. All those thoughts raced through Bonnie's mind as she stared longingly at the broad shoulders of the beloved, childhood friend who tended to the fire, ensuring she would not be cold as she finished the last gown.

I could be happy with you, she knew, without a shadow of a doubt. But how could she encourage him to ask for her hand, when she did not know if he felt the same way? All of her fragile hopes were built on a foundation of sand, constructed by Alice's fleeting suggestion that William had an affection for Bonnie. If Alice was wrong, however, Bonnie feared that mentioning marriage might ruin the friendship she cherished. And as Alice was but twelve years of age, with a head full of dreams and fairy-tales, it was very possible that she was mistaken.

"Now, dear Bonnie," William said, standing up, "shall we begin our last march to the finishing line?"

Bonnie forced a smile. "I suppose we must."

Yet, as she took to her position by the *Singer,* she had to wonder—how could it possibly be the end?

***

That evening, the sky black and starless beyond the dusty windows, Bonnie sat in the centre of the shop on a stool she had carried in from the back room, and watched the empty street as she sipped from a fresh bowl of hot soup. Alone, she held a private wake, mourning the loss of her father's mind and the shop he had adored with all of his heart, surrounded by an eerie congregation of mannequins and vacant shelves and display tables that no longer had anything to display.

William had returned home to his mother an hour prior, and Bonnie had not yet mustered the strength of spirit to mount the stairs and tell her own mother that it was all done. No more orders, no more work, no more beautiful gowns to sew and admire, no more lively chatter to chase off the biting cold, no more dreams of wearing her own gown, made by her father, at some fancy ball or another.

She had never truly known what she would do with her life, only that she would make something of herself, but even that seemed impossible now. Survival would take priority over everything else and, as of yet, she did not know how they were going to survive.

Bringing the bowl to her lips to sup the last dregs, her brow furrowed at the sight of two men halting on the opposite side of the road. They wore dark greatcoats, their hats shrouding their faces in darkness, and though she could not see their eyes, she sensed they were looking right at her.

A moment later, they crossed the street.

A dull knock thudded on the door. Bonnie knew she had been seen, but fear held her frozen upon the stool, the bowl still poised against her lips. A second knock echoed into the shop.

"Miss Acklam, I know you are there," a somewhat familiar voice called out.

Trembling, Bonnie set down the soup bowl and, smoothing out the creases in her pale blue skirts and adjusting the ruffled collar of her chemise, she headed for the door. With a breath, she opened it, bracing for more than an icy gust of wind.

"Mr. Penwortham, this is an unexpected surprise," she said, with all the courtesy she could muster for the landlord who undoubtedly held their safety and comfort in the palm of his hand.

The landlord was a tall, reedy fellow with a face like a turkey; his nose a hooked beak, his eyes beady, his fleshy jowls wobbling whenever he spoke. Yet, despite his severe appearance, he had always been kind towards the Acklam family. Then again, that was when they had been making a secure income, famed throughout society. How much kindness would a landlord show towards a family that had become infamous almost overnight?

"I can't fathom how it would be unexpected, Miss Acklam," Mr. Penwortham replied, smiling thinly. "When rents are unpaid, it is customary for a landlord to pay a very expected visit."

Bonnie frowned. "I do not know what you mean, Mr. Penwortham. The rents *have* been paid. My mother assured me of it."

"Might I speak with your mother? I would ask for your father, but I hear he will soon be committed to a sanatorium." Mr. Penwortham tutted as if the prospect disgusted him.

"My father will not be committed to anything of the kind," Bonnie retorted, her anger spiking. "He is unwell, that is true, but it is a passing sickness."

Mr. Penwortham raised an eyebrow and wagged a patronising finger at Bonnie. "It is unseemly for a young lady to lie, Miss Acklam. I am aware of your father's descent into madness, and whilst I can offer pity for that, I can offer no leniency for unpaid rents. Nothing has been paid to me for this month or the last, and I know I am not the only one seeking to recoup what is owed. The mercer is, by all accounts, owed a frightening sum by your father, as are the unhappy customers who are in possession of unfit garments."

"Pardon?" A chill beetled down Bonnie's spine.

"Fortunately," Mr. Penwortham continued without answering, "we have happened upon a solution that will ensure that your father doesn't find himself in debtors' prison. I have a gentleman here who wishes to purchase the shop and apartments and has agreed to pay for your father's debts in addition. Of course, there is a proviso..."

Bonnie's attention was drawn to the other gentleman, who stood behind Mr. Penwortham. Removing his hat, the fellow stepped into the dim light of the shop's lamps, revealing himself. A gasp lodged in Bonnie's throat as she glared at the gentleman, for though she did not know his name, she knew him: he was the fellow that had spoken with William on the street, not long ago.

"Miss Acklam, I do wish we could be meeting in pleasanter circumstances," the gentleman had the gall to say, as he attempted to take her hand. "I am Mr. Shannon, of Shannon & Company fine tailoring. Perhaps, you have heard of me?"

Bonnie recoiled from his reaching hand, stumbling further back into the shop as the pieces slotted together in her mind. She knew the name "Mr. Shannon" very well indeed, for he had long been her father's greatest competitor when it came to dressing gentlemen. Once upon a time, the wretch had endeavoured to dip his toe into dressmaking, but no one had requested any commissions. As such, he had been forced to paint over the part of his sign that said "dressmaking," returning to his usual trade of tailoring and gentlemen's attire.

"I see that you have," Mr. Shannon said with a sly grin.

"Out!" a piercing scream frightened Bonnie out of her skin. "Get out!"

Bonnie whirled around in time to see a blur racing past her with a rolling pin in hand, brandishing it at the two gentlemen who dared to trespass. Her mother had come to the rescue, but Bonnie sensed it was much too late for that.

"You told me the rents had been paid," she said quietly, her heart cracking as she looked upon her mother's wild-eyed, frantic face. "You swore we had months, Mama."

Her mother winced as if she had been struck. "We will have months, darling. As I have already told Mr. Penwortham here; he shall have his rents when the bolts of silk and satin are sold. As for that nonsense about my husband owing an extraordinary sum to the mercer—it is balderdash! He owes nothing.

The rare silk he ordered was never collected, and if it was not collected, there can be no debt for there was no exchange made. Indeed, I have it on good authority that the ship bringing the silk sank on its voyage, so how can my husband be responsible for the expense of goods that never made it to our shores?"

"The mercer says otherwise," Mr. Shannon interjected, his lip curling.

"Then the mercer is a liar!" Bonnie's mother raged, shaking her rolling pin as the gentlemen attempted to move closer. "Bonnie, fetch William—he knows precisely what was ordered. We shall all venture to the mercer's this evening and ask to see the silk that supposedly arrived, when I know it did not!"

Bonnie made to retreat into the workshop, to steal out of the back door, but Mr. Shannon's voice held her in place. "That shan't be necessary, Mrs. Acklam. Perhaps, you are right about the silk. However, the mercer will not take any of the bolts you have in your possession." He paused, smiling. "I, on the other hand, will purchase them from you. With what I am willing to offer, I am certain you will be able to find comfortable lodgings elsewhere, for a while at least."

"Have you asked the mercer not to purchase our wares? Have you contrived this, so we have no choice but to accept your measly offer?" Bonnie's mother accused, her voice dripping venom. Indeed, for a moment, Bonnie feared that her mother might actually swing the rolling pin at Mr. Shannon's head... and she would not have blamed her mother if she had.

Mr. Shannon shrugged. "Being associated with the dressmaker who ruined a Countess's reputation has more to do with his hesitancy. I have contrived nothing. I have only the greatest respect for your husband, but as he is unfit to continue, I am coming to your door to make this merciful offer. You will not receive better."

"Mrs. Acklam," Mr. Penwortham said, in a softer voice, "I would urge you to accept. Either way, I will be forced to evict you a fortnight hence, considering your unpaid rents. After all, if what Mr. Shannon says is true, I see no possible way in which you could pay what is owed by then."

But Bonnie's mother was not listening to the landlord; her furious gaze fixed upon Mr. Shannon. "You have no respect for my husband. You've never held the smallest jot of respect for him. All these years, you have been bitterly jealous, doin' everythin' in your power to try and thwart him. Each time you've failed, you've grown more twisted and resentful. You're naught but a vulture circlin' carrion, come to pick the bones of us dry! I'd wager you laughed yourself hoarse when you heard of me husband's misfortune. I'd wager you've orchestrated it all. Aye, I wouldn't be surprised if it was you who tampered with the Countess's gown in the first place, to ensure me husband would be ruined!"

Mr. Shannon stared at Bonnie's mother as if the woman was quite mad. Perhaps, she was, and with good reason.

"We will find a way, Mr. Penwortham," Bonnie interjected quickly, keeping one eye upon the rolling pin, in case her mother really did batter Mr. Shannon with it.

The landlord sighed and shook his head. "I have given ample opportunity for arrangements to be made, and I have not seen a single coin of payment. I sent countless letters to Mr. Acklam, at a time when I was in a more amenable mood, but all were ignored."

"What has he offered you?" Bonnie's mother spat at the landlord. "I spoke with you not a week ago, and you told me that you would accept a smaller sum from the sale of the fabrics, until we could recover from the slander that has been spread around this city. What changed, Mr. Penwortham? What has this wretched creature offered you, that you would turn your back on loyal tenants like us?"

"Money that is owed," Mr. Penwortham said simply. "I can't wait for the impossible, Mrs. Acklam. Your husband and his business will never recover, or so I am told. As such, I must protect my assets. In truth, I find your behaviour rather disappointing, for Mr. Shannon is providing *you* with your only opportunity to emerge from this debacle with some coin in your pockets."

Mr. Shannon tilted up his chin, puffed and proud. "I would urge you to consider my proposal of purchasing what remains of Mr. Acklam's wares. Let me help you. Do not allow stubbornness and pride to make the road ahead that much more difficult." He bowed his head and with a sharp, "I bid you a good evening, Mrs. Acklam, Miss Acklam," he turned on his heel and left the shop, likely before Bonnie's mother truly exploded with rage and ended up guilty of murder.

"I am sorry it has come to this," Mr. Penwortham said with a weary sigh. "I wish I could say it is the first time that I have seen something of this ilk come to pass, but... you are not the first to fall upon hard times and I doubt you shall be the last. I am truly sorry for it, but I can't fix what has been broken. So, please, as a long-standing friend of you and your family, do as Mr. Shannon has asked, for all of your sakes."

Tipping his hat, he followed Mr. Shannon out into the shadowed street, where they blended into the darkness as if they were born of it. Indeed, Bonnie had always suspected that if the Devil were to come knocking upon her door, he would come dressed in a fine suit with a pleasant smile, to trick her out of her immortal soul. Mr. Shannon did not want to help; he wanted to possess everything that Bonnie's father had owned, rubbing that final handful of salt into the wound after their years of rivalry.

"Of all the despicable, vile, blood-sucking vipers I have encountered..." her mother hissed, huffing out furious breaths as her body trembled from head to toe, overcome by violent rage.

"A viper he may be, but that doesn't mean he isn't right," Bonnie replied, clasping a hand to her chest to stop her heart from breaking. "If the mercer won't buy from us, he's our only hope of gathering a few nuts and berries for the winter ahead."

Her mother looked like she wanted to slap some sense into her daughter, but as Bonnie held her ground, tears welling in her eyes, her mother lowered her rolling pin and swept Bonnie into her arms. Holding each other tightly, they collapsed into one another, embracing for dear life, mourning together in the cold and draughty shop that was, in essence, no longer theirs. Their tears dripped onto each other's shoulders; the only warmth they could hope for, with their coffers almost empty.

"You must still go to the mercer tomorrow, with William," her mother urged, her voice thick with grief. "I won't believe a word that comes out of their treacherous mouths unless you hear it for yourself, from the mercer *him*self."

Bonnie froze in her mother's embrace, feeling no familiar rush of joy as she heard William's name spoken. Instead, each syllable wrapped around her throat like bony fingers, squeezing tight. In the unpleasantness, she had forgotten her dearest friend and tentative beloved, and how she had first come to know the face of Mr. Shannon.

William could not look me in the eyes... Bonnie remembered, her heart lurching into her throat, her stomach churning until a burning climb of acid clawed towards the back of her mouth, threatening to eject the soup she had been drinking earlier.

"Forgive me, Mama," she said in a hurry, pulling away from the life-raft that she dearly wished to cling onto, for if her suspicions turned out to be true, then she would find herself floating away upon rougher seas, in a much deadlier storm than she had anticipated. "There is something I must tend to. I shan't be long."

Her mother frowned. "Where are you goin'?"

"I'll... explain when I return," Bonnie promised, grabbing her cloak from the coat-stand.

At the door, her mother seized her by the wrist in an attempt to keep her from leaving. "It is bitterly cold outside, Bonnie. You will catch your death. Whatever it is, it can be seen to in the mornin'. For tonight, let's all... pretend that everythin' is well and no trouble has befallen us. I'll even bake us a cake—I think we've some butter and sugar left somewhere."

Nothing would have made Bonnie happier than to stay with her family in the beautiful apartments upstairs, putting on a performance of the simpler, more joyful times that now seemed like they belonged to a different life. More than anything, her aching heart longed to pull Alice into her arms, so she could hold her little sister and protect her from their uncertain future. But first, she had to know... she had to know if the man she cherished, the man she had grown up with, the man she had hoped would suggest marriage, the man she had grown to adore beyond friendship, was a stranger who had stabbed her in the back. A man who had been twisting the knife, whilst pretending to embrace her.

Chapter Seven

"How do you know him? Why were you talking to him on the street, when you claimed he was just your mother's acquaintance?" Bonnie did not pause to explain herself as the door to William's lodgings opened, and he blinked at her with sleepy, red eyes that he rubbed with his knuckles.

His mouth stretched in a yawn. "Who? You'll have to begin again; your words are running too fast for me to keep pace." He squinted past her shoulder at the ice-slicked cobbles. "What hour is it? Did you walk here alone?" His voice transformed from barely awake to deeply concerned in the jump of a heartbeat.

"How do you know Mr. Shannon?" Bonnie ignored the rest of his questions, the heat of her nervous anger keeping her warm for the time being.

William's eyes widened and his head turned away sharply: a sure sign of guilt if ever Bonnie had seen one. "He's... an acquaintance of my mother, as I said."

"Yet, you have never mentioned him before. I would think it might be important to mention that your mother's acquaintance is also the bitter rival of my father. Unless, of course, none of that is true, which I suspect it is not," Bonnie shot back, her words veined with crackling regret. Regret that she had trusted William. Regret that he could hurt her, after all they had endured together over the years that they had known one another. Regret that she had not been mistaken, after all.

William dropped his chin to his chest as he leaned against the doorjamb, like he could not hold up the weight of his shame any longer. "My mother worked for him when she was a younger woman, and he was the overseer at the seam," he explained in a rasping, pained tone.

"When she first took ill, he visited from time to time, bringing food or coin or medicine. I... have often wondered why that was, but those visits were a rarity; I promise you. In truth, I did not realise he was *that* Mr. Shannon until very recently, so I had no cause to mention it as I did not know. I have always known him as James."

"How recently?" Bonnie's voice quavered. "Did you know who he really was when you went to speak with him, outside the shop?"

William closed his eyes, grimacing. "Yes."

"Did you know of his wicked schemes?" Bonnie pressed, balling her hands into fists so she could not smack him or pull him to her, if only to feel a comfort she doubted she would ever feel again.

William's eyes shot open. "Schemes?"

Bonnie rushed through the abridged version of the encounter she had just experienced on the shop's doorstep, colouring the cruel tale with her own aspersions as she did so. "I suspect that he has seized this opportunity to ruin my father, and has orchestrated every wretched thing that has befallen the Acklam name. Even you thought it strange that the Countess had not come to be recompensed for her torn gown.

Perhaps, she was already compensated for the incident, before it even happened." Her nostrils flared, her rage hot in her chest. "Tell me you knew nothing of Mr. Shannon's plan to take everything and leave us with no choice but to bow our heads and accept the pittance he will offer for what is left."

"Bonnie, I would *never* do that to you," William said, after a long, strained pause; their eyes locked in a heated conflict. "If I had known, I would have told you. I would have sought to prevent it. You know me, Bonnie. You know I would do anything for you."

"Perhaps, like everyone else, you thought it might be the best bargain we could hope for," Bonnie retorted, her voice hitching as tears clogged her throat and crept up into her eyes, threatening to spill. "Perhaps, you thought you *were* helping us by helping him. You seemed awfully friendly when I saw you talking to one another."

William stepped out of the door, reaching for her hand. She staggered back, a twisted mirror image of him, shuffling further away with every approach he attempted to make. Her numb fingers longed to close around his, holding his hands tightly until the nightmare faded and some warmth returned to her chilled bones, but she feared that if she so much as touched him, her resolve would crumble.

"Bonnie, you must believe me—had I known, I would have told you. I want to help you, that is true, but not by selling your family's worth to another," he insisted, his brow creasing in a particular kind of sorrow that stung deep in Bonnie's heart. It was akin to an innocent man on trial begging to be believed. Yet, in her mind, William had been found with blood on his hands.

"You are lying to me," she rasped, choking out each word. "I *do* know you, William, so I know when you are hiding something. What are you not saying?"

William swept a hand through his golden-brown hair, the colour of summer chestnuts, his fingertips ruffling the silky strands. "He—Mr. Shannon—*did* offer me a position at his business, and… when I left you earlier, I *did* go to him and accept his proposal of work. But I did not know that business was your father's. I assumed it would be his shop on the other side of the city. I swear to you, if I had had any notion that he meant to steal what was yours, I would not have agreed!"

"You... agreed to work for him?" Bonnie's head swam; her palms clammy, her skin prickling with cold sweat, as if she might faint.

William tried once more to take her hand. "I have my mother to think of, Bonnie. I can't be without employ." He gripped his hand into a fist when she would not allow him to touch her, his face twisting in pain. "But I promise, I knew nothing of any scheme. I... thought he was doing me a kindness, but perhaps... perhaps, I have been somewhat naïve. Please, don't hate me for that. I didn't know," he gasped, tears shining in his own eyes. "I didn't know."

"I see," was all Bonnie could find it in her heart to say, as she took another step away from the handsome, sweet, charming young man that she no longer recognised.

If he had not known of Mr. Shannon's rivalry with her father when he accepted the offer of employment, perhaps she could have understood, but if he had accepted earlier that evening as he had said, then he knew full well who Mr. Shannon was. Indeed, anyone with a smidgen of sense might have suspected foul play, and William was no mooncalf.

"Bonnie, come inside," William urged, hissing as his bare feet touched the icy ground. "Let us have some tea and we can speak of this in a calmer fashion. You are angry; I understand that. You are upset, as anyone would be. But, please, come and sit by the fire and let me explain further. The last thing I want is to hurt you, or make you feel like I've... betrayed you in some manner."

Bonnie levelled her gaze at him, struggling not to immediately forgive the man she adored. Two tiny lanterns of desperation glinted in his gentle, green eyes, imploring her to come closer to him, to accept his invitation to step into the warmth of his lodgings.

But she could not show weakness now, not with the memory of Mr. Shannon's smug face haunting her thoughts, and the vision of that wretch laughing and smiling with William in the street, clapping him on the back like they were dear friends.

"Let me ask you this," she said stiffly, her heart shrivelling as all hope was sucked from it. "Now that you know what Mr. Shannon has done, and what I suspect he might have done, will you still work for him? Indeed, will you still work for him in the place of your former employment, where we toiled diligently, side-by-side, these past weeks? Will you work in that place, knowing what we have lost by Mr. Shannon's theft? Will you be able to sit at the workbench where I have watched you and admired you since you began your apprenticeship, whilst the apartments upstairs—where I used to prepare your luncheon and endless tea trays just to gain your attention for a short while—will have another family residing within it?"

William's face fell, as she had known it would, for she already knew the answer he would give. He had made his decision, and whilst she understood why, she could not accept it.

"I thought I loved you, William," she whispered, before she could stop herself. "I had hoped you might... save me and my family in another way, inheriting my father's business. To see you at the helm—a man my father trusted— would have soothed the sting of everything that has befallen us, of late. I see, now, that I was mistaken in so many ways."

William's eyes widened to the whites as he edged closer to her on his bare feet, hissing through each step which must have felt like shards of glass prodding into his skin. He stretched out his hand towards her, beckoning for her to come to him, but she would not. He had made his decision, and so had she.

"Bonnie, I—"

"You have said all I wish to hear," Bonnie interrupted, backing away. "And what you have not said is confession enough of your intentions. I wish you well, William. I wish your mother good health. Meanwhile, I hope that you will pray for the health of my own family, and that you think of us from time to time, whilst you are sitting in the workshop of the man who ruined us—no, the workshop of my father, who rescued you from destitution and kept your mother alive when you were certain she would die."

Having hurled those vicious barbs, feeling the cut of them in her own throat and heart, Bonnie turned sharply and hurried away before William could see the tears streaming down her cheeks, and the regret that beat like a hot, feverish drum in her temples. It was not his fault. She knew that, but it did nothing to lessen the betrayal that slithered through her veins, transforming the man she cherished into a man she hoped to never see again.

Turning a corner, almost slipping on the ice, she thought she heard her name, splintering through the night air in a strangled cry... but she decided it was just the wind, and pressed on through the darkness, her tears freezing on her skin as her breath billowed in wispy clouds. The cold was unyielding, yet it was nothing compared to the numbness that sapped the last promise of warmth from her bones. William had been that promise, and it had been broken.

As such, she had no desire to return home immediately—or, rather, to the place that they could only call home for another fortnight, before Mr. Shannon came to claim what was now his. On sluggish feet, Bonnie made her way toward a jagged fang of land where the River Ouse met the River Foss; the two watery serpents weaving through the city, dividing it but never conquering it, even when the water levels rose.

There, upon the fang's very peak, she sat down and dangled her legs over the side of the jutting stone, which tongued out into the water like a pier. In the springtime, wildflowers grew there in abundance, and the city's residents wandered in the sunshine, inhaling the rich perfumes that wafted from the small, dainty flowers. Butterflies and bees made pilgrimages in the summer, filling the air with a comforting hum, but in the winter, everything was stripped bare of its beauty.

The trees were skeletal, the bushes sparse, the browned plants looking like they might never flower again, and no one wandered for the sake of wandering if they could help it when the temperature dropped.

In the anaemic glow of a streetlamp, recently ignited, Bonnie watched the water sparkle, making a wish upon each glinting wavelet—the same wish, over and over: *Please let this be a terrible dream. Please let me awaken to the morning of my birthday. Please let us be saved.* But if the joined rivers heard, they did not answer.

Before long, numb to the bone, Bonnie wondered if she was becoming part of the black night, if it was showing mercy by drawing her into the shadows, helping her to disappear so she would not have to face the future.

She could feel herself fading; the bitter cold replaced by a strange warmth that seeped through her veins, making her sleepy. Indeed, she thought it might be pleasant to curl up where she was and let that desire to slumber overwhelm her. Whether or not she would awaken; it was no more of an uncertainty than the rest of what awaited her and her family.

Alice would be heartbroken, her mind whispered in a plea. *You must not give up. You must be a pillar for your mother and sister.* But as the warm, numbing sensation took over, she struggled to claw her way back to the surface of reality, sinking deeper into the abyss where nothing mattered.

"Bonnie?" a soft voice urged, as arms slipped around her. "Bonnie, you can't rest here."

She was aware of being lifted, but not by whom. The voice was gentle and familiar, making her tired heart soar, but as she leant into the heat of her saviour's body, resting her head upon broad shoulders, she could not fight slumber anymore. Closing her eyes, she did precisely what they had told her not to: she rested, feeling safe... if only for a short while.

Chapter Eight

Bonnie spent the last fortnight that the Acklams would ever spend in their pleasant apartments by languishing in bed, feverish and trembling, tended to by a worried mother who was on the brink of exhaustion with every waking moment. Alice helped where she could, for there was no longer any hope of keeping the state of the family's future from her. As such, she had been withdrawn from the Grammar School, taking on the role that Bonnie once occupied: fetching water, helping to cook, cleaning every room, and caring for those who were in need of it.

"Are you going to die, Bon-Bon?" Alice asked one evening, as the day of the family's departure grew nearer. Two more nights, and their home would belong to Mr. Shannon. Two more nights, and they would be cast out onto the street, so perhaps it was a twisted blessing that Bonnie was too sick to dwell upon it.

Bonnie stirred from her delirious slumber, blinking open bleary eyes. "Hmm?"

"Are you and Papa going to die?" Alice repeated, perched on the edge of the bed, staring down at the dusty floor.

Bonnie twisted beneath the coverlets, to turn closer to her sister. "I... hope not."

"Mama is so... scared, Bonnie," Alice whispered, her voice tight and terrified. "Everything we own is in crates and boxes, and she... shouts at me when she can't find something."

Bonnie struggled to sit up, her head pounding. "I will... help. Give me your... hand."

"Mama says you're to stay in bed," Alice insisted, refusing to take her sister's shaky, outstretched hand. "Why did you go out into the cold, Bonnie? I overheard Mama and William when he brought you back. He said he found you by the river. I've never seen Mama go so pale. What were you doing, Bonnie?"

"Thinking," Bonnie replied, for it was half the truth at least.

"William has visited you every day. He's been bringing food and medicine," Alice said, suddenly clamping a hand over her mouth. "Oh... I wasn't supposed to mention that. I don't know why, but he didn't want you to know. Did he tell you that he loved you, and you refused him?"

Bonnie mustered a thin smile. "No, dearest Alice, nothing like that."

In her fever dreams, Bonnie had been gifted with visions of a future that would never come to pass; her and William, married and blissfully happy, surrounded by sturdy and healthy children with rosy cheeks; the couple working together each day in the workshop of Acklam & Sons, having saved the shop from the brink of theft.

In those dreams, she had walked with William by the river in the heat of summer, inhaling the perfume of the wildflowers, pointing to the rarest butterflies that fluttered by.

And he had held her hand and kissed her softly, as she had always dreamed that he might, so in love with one another that it might passers-by smile and mutter enviously to their companions.

But they were just dreams, and when she awoke, perspiring and coughing and so hot she could not stand to be constrained by her own skin, she remembered—remembered what he had done, how he had betrayed her family, and that there would be no rescuing the shop from Mr. Shannon's greedy hands.

"He said you might be cross with him," Alice pressed. "Did you quarrel? Can't you be friends again, even if you can't love him?"

Bonnie winced. "It's not about love, Alice. I..." she trailed off, turning her back so her sister would not see the tears that threatened to spill. "I need to rest."

She felt the springs of the bed shift as Alice got up, and heard the soft, sad pad of footsteps as Alice retreated. At the bedchamber door, Alice paused, offering one last sentiment before she departed. "I wish things were different," she said, and closed the door.

As do I, Alice... my goodness, as do I. Squeezing her eyes shut, Bonnie let the tears come, soaking into the pillow beneath her head.

And in the darkness, she sobbed for what might have been, and everything they would soon lose forever, including the man she had hoped she would have at her side, in some capacity, for the rest of her life.

***

By the morning of the family's departure, Bonnie had recovered just enough strength to help carry some of their belongings to the cart that waited on the street outside the shop, in full view of all the jeering wretches who thought they were celebrating a comeuppance.

Many long-standing clients of Bernard Acklam's cursed his name, throwing torn garments onto the dirty ground, to the point where Bonnie was almost glad that her father had taken complete leave of his senses, for he did not deserve to be so reviled when all he had done, with the entirety of his life, was create beauty for those same people.

"Let them bay like stray dogs," Bonnie's mother hissed, as she brought the last crates down from the kitchen. The last boxes from a paradise they were leaving behind. "They will be sorry when Mr. Shannon ruins this establishment. They'll have to scream for the attention of a London dressmaker when they realise Mr. Shannon can't make gowns for toffee!"

Bonnie paused to catch her breath, just beside the door that led into the workshop. "Are we truly leaving everything behind for that monster?"

"Those are the terms," her mother replied bitterly. "He's given the coin for them already, by way of Mr. Penwortham. If I took so much as a scrap of silk, it'd be stealin'. Though, I've half a mind to take some anyway."

Bonnie noticed the victorious smirk upon her mother's face. "Have you?"

"Never you mind that." Her mother nudged Bonnie lightly in the arm, urging her toward the main door and the street beyond.

With the final boxes stowed away, Bonnie climbed into the back of the cart and wedged herself between a table and some chairs. Alice was already hemmed in by a cabinet and an armoire, the sisters left to endure the jeers and cries of the growing crowd whilst their mother returned inside for one last thing.

"Bernard Acklam ought to be in prison!" someone yelled.

"To think I ever bought aught from that charlatan!" another bellowed.

"You're lucky we didn't run you out of the city!" barked a third. "We should've burned you all to nothing!"

Unable to bear the vile onslaught, Bonnie twisted around to face the scowling throng. "When you're paying three times the cost for half the talent, I hope you all see the error of your ways! You'll be shouting and hollering to have him back, then, but it'll be too late for that! He didn't do one thing wrong, and this is how you repay him! You're despicable, every last one of you!"

The crowd writhed in fury, trying to surge closer to the cart to teach the wild-eyed girl a lesson. Bonnie stared them down, her fury more incendiary than any of theirs. Her hand itched for a rotten plum or a worm-ridden apple to throw, but there was nothing she could hurl back at them other than her words.

"This is all a wickedness of Mr. Shannon's creation!" she shouted. "He has stolen my father's livelihood. He has conjured all of this, and once you realise it, it will be too late to remedy it! He—"

Something struck her in the face, so hard it halted the words upon her lips. A sting webbed from the apple of her cheek down to her jaw, chased by a thick, warm liquid that trickled like a tear. Her hand came up to touch the injury, and when she looked at her fingertips, they were red with blood.

"Bonnie!" A figure shoved his way through the throng, clambering right up onto the cart though there was no room for him. He wrapped his arms tightly around her, using his body to protect her. "Bonnie, there is no use. They will tear you all apart if you rile them."

"So, I should stay silent?" she gasped, still shocked by the blow to her cheek; a rock or a stone, that was now somewhere among their belongings.

He held her tighter, and she did not attempt to push him away. He felt warm and safe, as he had always done, and as she buried her face in his chest, she wished more than ever that things were different.

She wished she had gone into his lodgings and taken tea with him, listening with a clear head to his reasoning instead of running off into the cold dark, almost freezing to death. She wished she had stayed to listen to what he might have said, what hopes he might have offered her, but too much time had gone by and now there was a strange distance between them that she could not traverse.

"I will write to you," William told her effusively. "And when I have made fortune enough to be... worthy of you, I will come to you. I will make all of this seem like a terrible nightmare. I promise it, Bonnie. By the time a year has passed, I will make everything good again. Endure for me, until then, and all will be well."

She pulled back. "What do you mean?"

"I must work to help my mother, that is true, but that is not my sole reason," he said, his eyes glittering with tears. "I always meant to ask you, Bonnie. I was always going to ask you. It was always you. I... just did not have the means, and still do not. But I will, and if I must spend the rest of my days earning your forgiveness for my... missteps, then I shall. As long as I can be at your side, I will do all I must."

Bonnie shook her head, confused. "The means for what?"

"You said you thought you loved me," he explained, somewhat shyly. "I have always loved you. I have loved you since I was a boy, and we were climbing trees and skating on the river in the winter. I will turn that love into a life for us, if you will have me a year from now."

Bonnie's eyes widened, her heart lurching as William suddenly winced; someone had thrown something at him. "But... you are working for *him*."

"I didn't know," he murmured, repeating what he had said when she stood in his doorway. "It is my hope that, in a year, you might have found it in your heart to forgive me. I will write to you with that same hope."

Bonnie's breath caught in her throat. "As long as Mr. Shannon is your employer, there is no hope for us." It was a lie, cresting on a wave of stubbornness that would not ebb. She wanted to promise her heart to him, then and there; she wanted to hold him and kiss him and swear to wait for a year, but the words would not come.

"I will solve this," he said with a confidence that disarmed her. "I do not yet know how, but I will. As soon as you reach your aunt, write to me so I know how to correspond with you. I promise, I will make everything right."

She wanted to believe him, she really did, but in a world like theirs, it was not easy to abandon good employment with a hearty income for the sake of something as fragile as love. In a year, he might have found someone else to divert his affections. In a year, he might have grown so accustomed to his income that he would not relinquish it for a lesser position. There were too many unknowns, holding Bonnie back from saying she would wait with an eager heart.

Just then, Bonnie's mother appeared at the door of Acklam & Sons with Bernard at her side; his arm around his wife's shoulder, leaning all of his meagre weight upon her once-robust frame.

The crowd exploded into a volatile rage as rocks and stones began to fly. Without a word to Bonnie, William let go of her and leapt down from the cart, moving to protect Bernard from the onslaught. Bonnie had never felt a pain like it; the aching absence of William's arms around her.

"Rot in Hell!" Bernard seethed at the crowd, barking expletives that made Bonnie's eyes widen in horror. Who was this man who barely even resembled her father anymore? Who was this stranger?

William scooped Bernard up into his arms and carried the filthy, emaciated man to the cart, slotting him in beside a cramped pile of kitchen chairs. All the while, stones hailed down, bouncing off the cart and the Acklam family's belongings, shattering glass and ceramics, adding insult to injury.

Meanwhile, Bonnie's mother climbed up onto the driver's bench and seized hold of the reins, her body trembling. A stone hit her squarely between the shoulder blades, but she did not even flinch. Instead, she snapped the reins, and the equally threadbare horse began to pull the cart forward.

For a while, stones and rocks continued to strike the departing cart, but the crowd seemed to be satisfied that the contagion was leaving their fine city and did not attempt to follow. Indeed, the only one who ran alongside was William, his athletic figure making easy work of keeping pace.

"I will write every day," he promised, gazing up at Bonnie. "I will visit if I can. Sheffield is not so far away."

Bonnie reached out her hand, and he grasped her outstretched fingers. "You should forget me," she said.

"Never. It has always been you, Bonnie. Nothing will change that for me," he urged, suddenly jumping up onto the back of the cart. Balancing precariously, he leaned down to where she sat among the cabinets and bed frames, and kissed her. A soft, sweet kiss, his lips jolted by the cartwheels on the cobblestones.

Despite her stubbornness, she kissed him back, though it was like a promise written on thin paper in a downpour. The year to come might crumble it to wet fragments of nothing, the ink running until neither of them could remember what it said.

"I love you, Bonnie," he told her, jumping back down, his hand still holding hers.

Too choked to respond, she held onto that precious hand for as long as she could, until the crush of people and other carriages and carts prevented him from staying by her side. He darted toward the safety of the pavement, but his gaze did not leave hers until they had turned a corner, blocking him from view.

And as the cart pressed on toward the edge of the city, where they would finally reach a point of no return, she wished she had told him that she loved him in return.

She wished she did not have to leave. She wished they had told one another of their feelings sooner, so all of this might have been avoided. But it was too late now. All she could do was look forward to his letters, and hope that his promise could withstand the storm to come.

"So, you do love him," Alice whispered with a sad smile.

Bonnie closed her eyes, fighting back tears. "Yes, dear Alice, I believe I do."

But love could not stop their family from losing everything, it could not undo what had been done, nor could it halt them from continuing their journey to Sheffield: a stark, industrial town that Bonnie had only heard terrible things about, a world away from the beautiful city she had known her entire life. Against her will, a new beginning beckoned.

Chapter Nine

The Acklam family arrived in the Neepsend district of Sheffield under the cover of winter darkness, the feeble streetlamps refusing to make the last stretch of their journey easier as the cart rumbled through cramped streets. A few curious observers watched from street corners, whispering between puffs of a pipe in a manner that made Bonnie nervous, but it was the silence that made her more uneasy. True, it was a bitterly cold evening, but where was everyone? There should have been children running wild in the streets, women chattering to their neighbours, men laughing with friends, everyone seeking company to either steal or share some warmth.

"I don't like it," Alice whispered, reaching for Bonnie's hand. "It is... cold."

Bonnie understood that her sister was not just talking about the weather. The rows upon rows of back-to-back terraced houses were soulless and bleak, crushed together to fit as many into one patch of land as possible, without so much as a yard to allow breath between the houses and those who resided within. Judging by the quantity of shadows that passed across each window—some covered with threadbare curtains; others, a couple of sheets from a newspaper—there were likely several families jammed into each house, too.

We were so very lucky, Bonnie lamented in frightened silence, thinking of the comfortable apartments in York and the opportunities that she and Alice had enjoyed for so long.

She had always understood their privilege and fortune, but she had not known quite how much she would miss it, now that it was gone. In a way, their departure from York had not even seemed real until that moment, navigating the narrow streets of a strange district in the dark, realising that they would never go back to that pleasant, tree-lined street in York or wake up again in the only home she had ever known.

"There it is," Bonnie's mother announced, leading the cart to the very end of the cobbled street. A thin stretch of barren land, scattered with the waste of the neighbourhood, stood between the last terrace and the River Don, which glinted menacingly in the darkness.

Bonnie's mother brought the cart to a standstill, and the door of that last terraced house opened, revealing a pale, weary face belonging to a thin woman in a threadbare dress and a dirtied pinafore. What could only be described as a horde of children pushed past her, rushing up to the horse and the cart, climbing right into the latter to see if there was anything that caught their eye.

"Forgive them," sighed the woman. A vaguely familiar woman. "It's been an age since they've had visitors. They'll tire soon enough." She did not sound convinced, as she walked up to the driver's bench and helped Bonnie's mother down. The two women embraced as only sisters, long separated, could.

"I've missed you, Katie," Bonnie's mother whispered.

"As I've missed you," her sister, Katie, replied. "Now, I know we don't have much, and I know it'll take a while for you lot to settle, but we've food and a roof that don't drip too much, and you'll be comfortable enough."

Bonnie's mother hurriedly dabbed at her eyes. "Thank you, sister."

"No thanks needed, Clara. I'm just glad that, for once, I can help you," Katie said solemnly, before snapping her fingers at one of the little boys who was flagrantly riffling through a drawer of valuables. "Get down from there, all of you! That's no way to welcome your cousins and your aunt and uncle! Show some bloody manners!"

Like rats escaping a sinking vessel, the seven children retreated from their search, gathering around their mother like they were preparing for a Sunday sermon. There were five boys and two girls, all younger than Bonnie, though one of the girls seemed close in age to Alice. The rest were younger.

"Peter is at the steelworks all night," Katie explained, "so you'll be meetin' him tomorrow, but make yourselves at home. Meanwhile, these are my brood: Little Peter, John, Luke, George, Christopher, Annabelle, and Edith."

The children nodded their heads as they were named, though Bonnie suspected it would take some time for her to remember who was who, particularly with the boys.

"Is that cart ours now, Ma?" one of the boys asked.

Katie smiled sadly. "No."

"No?" Bonnie parroted, looking to her mother for answers.

Bonnie's mother sighed and stroked the nose of their loyal horse. "We've to sell both horse and cart, Bonnie. We've no use for either now."

Bonnie wanted to protest, wanted to hold onto some semblance of their past life, but she knew there was no point. With no coin left in the coffers, they would likely have to sell everything they had brought with them. Indeed, it had not occurred to Bonnie until that moment that that was why they had brought everything with them to a terraced house that could barely accommodate them. It was not for keeping, but for selling.

"Come on in out of the cold," Katie urged. "We've the entire house to us-selves. One of only a few on the street who can say that," she added proudly, ushering everyone inside.

Bonnie's mother paused, glancing at Bernard, who had fallen asleep amongst the furniture. "Will everythin' be safe?"

"Oh aye, no one will touch anythin'," Katie replied, frowning. "Is Bernard comin' in or are you goin' to leave him as he is?"

Bonnie's mother hesitated. "I'll leave him for now. He'll not get cold, wrapped in all of those blankets, and I'd known where he's to sleep before disturbin' him. He's… not been himself, as I told you in my letters."

"It'll do him good to be around people," Katie insisted confidently, closing the door against the cold and the cart of memories that would soon be sold for the highest price.

The tour of the house was a short one, leaving Bonnie dumbstruck as to how so many people could fit inside just four rooms. Indeed, how they could fit four more people inside those rooms. There were two rooms on the lower floor—one bedchamber, one kitchen—and two more bedchambers on the upper floor. The boys shared one, the girls shared another, and the lower bedchamber was for Katie and her husband.

"Your girls don't mind sharin' with mine, do they?" Katie asked, as everyone reconvened in the kitchen.

Bonnie shook her head politely, though Alice looked horrified. "Not at all, Aunt Katie."

"And you and Bernard will be in with me and Peter, or you can make yourselves a corner of this here kitchen if you prefer. I don't know what'd be best, under the circumstances," Katie continued, chewing her lower lip.

Bonnie's mother paled. "I think it best if we take a corner of the kitchen."

"As you like," Katie replied, seeming just a little bit relieved. "In the mornin', Alice can go on to the school with my lot. For you and Bonnie— there's work for you up at the steelworks. You'll come along with me. It pays well and though it ain't exactly a thrill, it's honest work."

Bonnie's heart sank, realising that all of her grand dreams of becoming something of merit, something of her choice, had truly come to a grinding halt. The Acklam family were no longer of the middle class, but of the working class.

"Is there nothin' for my Bonnie at the seam, perhaps?" her mother asked hurriedly. "She's a gifted seamstress."

Katie raised a curious eyebrow. "Well, I can ask around, but I can't promise aught."

"I will do whatever is necessary," Bonnie insisted, though her heart did not agree.

Katie smiled. "You've a strong lass there, Clara. She'll do just fine in Sheffield, I'd wager." She paused. "Now, let us get you all fed and watered, then we can start with puttin' all of... that on the cart into the bedchamber. Peter won't mind it stayin' there 'til you can sell it."

Just then, a wail cut through the air, bone-chilling and blood-curdling, like a wounded animal. Bonnie's mother winced as everyone looked toward the windows, no doubt wondering what on Earth could make such a sound. Of course, Bonnie, Alice, and their mother knew.

"I'll tend to him," Bonnie's mother said softly. "You get your bellies filled and go on to bed."

Bonnie paused. "Are you certain?"

"Of course, love," her mother replied, heading out of the door.

In that instant, Bonnie had to wonder if it might have been better for her father if he had died in the apartments he had cherished, above the shop he had given his life and his passion to. For how could a man, toppled over the brink of insanity, possibly come to terms with the new condition of their lives? It was hard enough for those who still had their faculties.

What have I become? she pondered, horrified that she could have considered such an awful thing. Yet, staring around at the coal-dust blackened windows and the suffocating kitchen where smoke billowed from a blocked flue, choking her throat, she could not tell herself that she was wrong. It *would* have been better if her father had not lived to see such times.

***

That night, huddled against the far wall of the girls' bedchamber with Alice sleeping soundly in her arms, Bonnie finally allowed her mask of courage to slip. Her cousins were also sleeping peacefully, their soft breaths filling the dirty, sour-smelling room, where black mould spiderwebbed in every corner and the ceiling—perhaps white once—had turned a permanent shade of brown. Bonnie envied them their ability to slumber without a worry, as the weight of hers pushed tears from her eyes, sending them down her cheeks in silent rivulets.

As quietly as she could, Bonnie sobbed into the flat pillow beneath her head, thinking of William and the flimsy promise of his kiss. It had happened so fast that she still wondered if she had dreamt it, but as she closed her stinging eyes and remembered, she felt the echo of his lips against hers. A soft graze, so powerful she was surprised it had not left some kind of imprint.

He will return for me. He will keep his promise, she told herself. *He will make something of himself, he will build his fortune, and then... he will pull me and my family from this pit we have found ourselves in.* All she had to do was wait a year. One year. Considering all she had already endured; how hard could that be?

"Do not forget me," she whispered against the mouldy-smelling pillow. "William, I beg of you— do not forget me."

For if he did, all hope would be lost.

Chapter Ten

Sheffield, March 1864

As the seasons began to change, and spring bloomed from the frosts of winter, Bonnie had also begun to flourish in the new beginning that life had dealt her. Like the scraps of fabric that her father used to save from his fine gowns and elegant tailoring, she had salvaged hope and happiness from the unfortunate situation, patching and sewing together a new existence until she had fashioned something that resembled contentment. It was not grand, it was not what she had always dreamed of, it was not easy, but it was enough to keep a smile upon her face and enough to make her get out of bed without argument.

"You're making the rest of us look lazy!" one of her friends at the steelworks, Bess, complained as the clock ticked down the last few minutes of their shift.

Bonnie grinned. "Either that, or you are."

"Eeh, the gall of ye!" Bess chuckled, pausing to splay out her fingers, bending and flexing them into fists. "I'll have you know I'm still sufferin' that rheumatism from winter."

Bonnie smiled. "There wasn't anything the matter with your hands when you were holding onto Davis McSwain yesterday."

"Bonnie Acklam, if I didn't adore the bones of you, I'd jab you with this here fork!" Bess cried, cackling as the other women on the assembly line rolled their eyes. It was common knowledge that Bess and Davis were sweethearts, though Bess seemed determined to pretend that it was a great secret.

Bonnie raised the fork she had been filing down, swiping it through the air like a skilled swordsman. "You'd have to get past my own fork first."

"Anyway, you can talk about me and Davis all you like, but I've seen those little love letters you've been hidin'," Bess teased, as she returned to filing off the jagged edges of the knives, forks, and spoons that came along the line from the main body of the steelworks: fine cutlery, destined for fine families in fine houses in fine districts where they would dine on fine food and not give a second thought to who had ensured they did not nick their tongues on sharp fragments of steel.

Bonnie shot her friend a warning look. "They are not love letters. They are letters from my dearest friend."

"Aye, and we all know what that means," Bess replied, flashing a wink that made Bonnie's cheeks flame with heat. Along the line of thirty women, soft chuckles could be heard that only added to the warmth of her skin.

Fortunately, Bonnie's mother and aunt had worked the night shift, and were at home French polishing furniture for some additional income: an idea that Bonnie's mother had had when it came to selling their worldly belongings.

An idea that had paid off, though it meant a never-ending cycle of work for all of them.

"They *are* from my dearest friend!" Bonnie insisted, her heart swelling at the thought of those sweet letters, so long and longed-for, brimming with words of unwavering affection and how much William missed her.

She looked forward to their twice-weekly arrival, always meeting the postman at the door so no one else would try to steal the letter and tease her mercilessly for its contents. After all, though her cousins were adorable and she had come to love each and every one, they could be little devils when they wanted to be. Although, as few of them could read well, she was certain that, even if they should steal her letter, they would not be able to understand what was written.

"A dear friend who ye're hopin' to marry," Bess replied, raising an eyebrow. "I know what it looks like when a lass is in love, and you're sick as a dog with it."

Bonnie rolled her eyes. "You've such a charming way with words."

"I *am* somethin' of a poet." Bess laughed, and as the women returned to their work, Bonnie could not help but offer a prayer of gratitude to the heavens for surrounding her with such good people.

She had been so afraid of Sheffield and of the steelworks and of the unknown, but, so far, she had been welcomed with open arms and made to feel as if she had always been there. Indeed, she no longer knew how she had coped with the relative silence of the apartments above the shop, for there was something truly wonderful about a house that was filled with joy and jokes and noise, and a bedchamber that carried the whisper of peaceful breaths and gentle snores. Meals were a beautiful sort of chaos, and evenings huddled around the kitchen fire, telling stories, singing, and sewing were something that gladdened her heart.

If only my father could be healed, I would never ask for anything more than I have, she thought, grimacing as a tiny filing of steel bit into her finger. She put her finger into her mouth, tasting the metal of her blood.

It was the only dark cloud in the blue skies of her new life: her father's sickness. At times, it permeated her fragile happiness like morning fog slithering up the banks from the river, turning the warmth of a crowded house cold. Other times, her new friendships and bonds and love for her cousins and aunt and uncle burned away that fog, helping her to block out the chill of it.

Perhaps, that was why she relished the noise of the terraced house on the banks of the River Don, for it helped her to block out the din of her thoughts and the crazed ravings of her beloved father.

"He seems... calmer," her mother often declared, whenever she and Bonnie stepped outside to take in some fresh air, their heads dizzy with the fumes of the polish and varnish they used for the furniture finishings. *"He sleeps through the night now."*

Bonnie did not have the heart to confess that she knew why her father slept through the night. She had seen the bottle of laudanum for herself, stashed at the back of the only cabinet from their apartments that had not been sold.

A cabinet with false bottoms and secret compartments, where Bonnie had also discovered two rolls of exquisite silk. After all, what was the alternative? If the laudanum eased her father's suffering and, in turn, her mother's, then how could she argue?

"Will Alice be waitin' for ye?" Bess asked, drawing Bonnie out of her private thoughts.

Bonnie shook her head. "Not today. My mother needed her home to finish some tables and chairs. Thought I might buy some barley sugars on the way, though, so she doesn't feel too sore about it."

"You spoil her," Bess said, with a warm smile. "Rightly, too. She's goin' to drag the lot of you from the mire of Sheffield when some fine, wealthy lad falls head over heels in love with her."

Bonnie chuckled. "She's twelve. She'll not be thinking about husbands and suchlike for years to come, with any luck."

Indeed, the only thing Alice could talk about for the past month was dancing ballet and singing with the girls' choir at the local church.

She had settled into life in Sheffield as if she had always been there, making friends at the drop of a hat, winning prizes at her school for English and arithmetic, and she loved nothing more than to play on the riverbank with her cousins, Annabelle and Edith.

The former was the same age as Alice, and the latter was only two years younger. Ever since Alice's arrival, the girls had formed a tightly knit trio, and while Bonnie sometimes envied their closeness, she would not have denied Alice that kinship.

In a strange way, everyone seemed happier. Even Bonnie's mother, Clara, was rarely without a smile on her face, always gossiping and laughing with Katie, or the other women on the street.

And though Bonnie wished her father was as he had once been, she had to wonder if her mother had finally found a purpose she did not know she had been missing, all these years. Either that, or Clara was merely trying to stay occupied and invested in the community around them, so she would not miss the life she used to have.

Just then, the bell rang for the end of the shift. Along the assembly line of filers and polishers and packers, the women stretched out backs that had been hunched for hours, and arms that ached from the repetitive movements, each one rising from their uncomfortable stools with a look of relief and satisfaction upon their faces.

"Are you coming for a sip of somethin' with us?" Bess asked, untying her pinafore and rolling it up to put in her carpet bag.

Bonnie shook her head. "Not tonight. I should get home to help my mother—the confectioner closes soon, and I don't want to return empty-handed."

"You and your sister are sweet enough," Bess teased. "Can't I tempt you?"

Bonnie smiled. "You're a terrible influence; has anyone ever told you that?"

"Listen to you and your fancy words. I don't even know what "influence" means." Bess grinned and slung her bag over her shoulder.

"You enjoy yourselves. I'll be getting teary-eyed and light-headed with polish fumes instead," Bonnie insisted, following Bess out of the large red-brick building where they spent their days and nights, depending on the shift.

Behind it stood the enormous factory and the hulking towers of the steelworks' furnace chimneys; the huge, brick cones concealing the long stone "pots" where pig iron and charcoal were packed in layers to begin the cementation process that would eventually create the raw steel.

From there, it was passed through to the rollers and the grinders and the filing cutters— men, boys, girls, women of all ages—that made all the cutlery and tools that then made their way to the final assembly and filing and packing lines.

Bonnie did not fully understand the process, but the smoke that billowed from the furnaces and the unyielding racket from within the factory conjured hellish visions.

Whenever she looked up at those chimneys, she reminded herself to be grateful that she had not ended up employed within those main factory walls. Indeed, she counted her blessings twice when she saw the lines of workers trailing out when their shift ended: dirty, sweat-drenched figures, some struggling to stay upright as they walked away from the heat and hard toil, exhausted beyond measure. There were, of course, some regulations in place to prevent children and women from working beyond a certain number of hours, but where mouths needed feeding and coin was desperately required, those regulations were often ignored by worker and overseer alike.

We are lucky, she told herself, not for the first time, as she hurried on toward the confectioner, hoping it had not yet closed for the evening.

***

"What are you eating so secretively? I can hear you eating," a voice accused from the doorway to the kitchen, where Bonnie, Alice, and their mother had gathered to enjoy some barley sugars before they took to their beds. It was a nightly delight that they enjoyed when everyone else had already retired; the three of them taking half an hour to sit before the fire and just be in one another's company before they also retired for the night. Sometimes, they had treats to share. Sometimes, stories. Sometimes, nothing but the comfortable silence of a family who loved one another dearly.

"Bernard?" Clara turned in alarm. "What are you doin' out of your bed? You're supposed to be restin'."

Bonnie's father shambled further into the kitchen, feeling his way along the floor with the toe of his bare foot. "All I do is rest. I'm tired of it!" he barked, his hand settling upon a chair which he proceeded to drag forward, getting closer to where the three ladies sat by the fireplace. "Where are my belongings? Where are my needles and threads and fabrics? Why can I never find a bloody thing when I need it? I've been searching for the key to the workshop, but I can't find it—where have you put it? Are you hiding it from me, like you're hiding those sweets you're eating?" He sat down a few paces from his wife and daughters.

"Would you like one?" Bonnie pushed the edge of the paper bag against her father's fingertips, fearful of his mood.

Her father snatched the bag out of her hand and stuffed a barley sugar into his mouth, sucking it with a boyish glee. "We should save some for tomorrow," he announced, cracking the boiled sweet with his teeth. The loud, splintering sound sent a shiver down Bonnie's spine.

"Tomorrow, darling?" Clara said. "What is tomorrow?"

Bernard cast a disbelieving look toward the wall; his wife sat in the opposite direction. "Why, it is dearest Bonnie's birthday! A young lady is only six-and-ten once." He paused. "And there will be cake, too. A pound cake. We must celebrate our daughter, darling. I am surprised you need to ask."

Bonnie and her mother exchanged a glance; the latter shook her head, as if to say, "I forgot to give him his medicine." It might have been shocking for the three ladies, to hear Bernard speak as if no time had passed at all, but it had been common enough in the bygone months that only Alice grimaced.

As much as possible, she had been sheltered from her father's ravings, but in a house so small and cramped, Bonnie and her mother could not always shield Alice from the painful truth— Bernard would never be cured of his blindness nor his mental affliction.

"I should have made a gown for you, dear Bonnie," he continued in a faraway voice. "We should see if it is not too late to have you debut. I have often wondered what I would make for you, if you were to enter into society. A gown of the rarest silk—a greenish blue, I think. Everyone would speak of it, everyone would clamour for one of their own, but I would never make another like it. Oh, I shall be famed for it; more famed than I have ever been." He suddenly shot up. "I must begin at once. Clara, where are the keys to the workshop? Where is William? He must be summoned immediately, for I cannot do this alone."

When he was in one of his gentler tempers, he always spoke as if it was Bonnie's birthday again, stuck in that day—stuck in the moment where his sight finally failed him, and he had to reveal the truth to her. It pained Bonnie to watch him relive that day, watch him pretend all was well and nothing had changed.

For when he spoke of the workshop and of making a new gown and of cake and treats and happy memories, his milky eyes seemed to brighten and his smile shone like a beacon of false hope, radiating from the emaciated, filthy, wretched changeling, as if her father was still somewhere inside, fighting to get out.

"Darling," Clara said carefully, "we've talked endlessly about this. You're not at the shop. You're not at the apartments. There's no key because there's no workshop. We're at my sister's in Sheffield."

Bernard snorted. "Nonsense. I can smell the silks and satins and crinoline from here. You mustn't jest, Clara; it's unkind."

"I'm not jestin', love," Clara replied with a choked sigh. It pained her, too. "We're at my sister's house in Neepsend. We had to leave, remember?"

Bonnie wished her father did not have to. She wished her mother did not have to break her heart, time and again, by reminding him. She wished she did not have to sit and watch the inevitable crumbling of her dear father's soul when he realised the truth and withdrew back into his shell, allowing the changeling to take the reins once more. Her muscles tensed, her breath lodged in her throat, as she waited for the explosion of his temper, remembering the days when she had never heard him so much as raise his voice to his wife or daughters.

What can we do to fix him? she pleaded in silence, but no one answered. No divine intervention or inspiration. Only the laudanum could dull the edges of his pain.

Clara gave Bonnie a subtle nod. With a heavy heart, Bonnie obeyed the instruction, rising quietly to her feet and tiptoeing to the farthest corner of the kitchen, where the cabinet stood, shrouded in shadow. As carefully as she could, she opened the right-hand drawer and felt for the false bottom. Lifting it, she took out the brown bottle of laudanum, hating that it had come to this.

"Very well, you've caught me," Clara said loudly, to cover the sound of Bonnie's tiptoeing feet. "I'm only teasin', my love, and you're right—it was unkind. But the hour is so late, darling. You can begin on Bonnie's gown in the mornin'. Now, why don't you have a little cup of warm milk, and we'll retire for the night?"

Bernard slowly sat back down in the chair. "That sounds nice."

"Doesn't it?" Clara's eyes glittered with tears as she quietly took the bottle from Bonnie and poured a hearty measure into the cup of warm milk that Clara had intended to him drink. "Here, dearest. Make sure to drink it all, else you'll never sleep."

Like a child, Bernard brought the cup to his lips and drank the contents down. When he was done, he wiped his mouth on the back of his dirtied sleeve and smiled contentedly. Bonnie watched, her heart dropping as that smile turned strange, his eyes glazing over, his body slumping in the chair.

"Help me," Clara instructed, moving to take one of Bernard's arms.

Bonnie and Alice both joined her, the three of them bearing his weight as they wielded him toward the storage cupboard beneath the stairs that had been transformed into a private sort of bedchamber for Clara and Bernard. Uncle Peter had insisted upon it after the noise of Bernard's babbling had made it impossible for him to sleep, and with his long shifts at the steelworks, he needed his rest. Giving up the space under the stairs had been a small price to pay.

Together, the three ladies managed to lay Bernard down upon the soiled and mouldering mattress, covering him with motheaten blankets as his eyelids fluttered. A moment later, he was fast asleep, breathing the shallow breaths of his laudanum-induced slumber. Bonnie hated that sound, terrified that, one day, the faint whisper of air moving in and out would fade altogether.

"Goodnight, Papa," Bonnie murmured, leaning down to kiss her father's brow. "Rest well."

He did not stir, already deep below the surface of consciousness.

"Goodnight." Alice echoed her older sister, though she did not kiss him. Instead, she held his hand and squeezed it gently, before clambering out of the cupboard and heading back to the kitchen.

Left alone, Clara peered up at her eldest daughter. "I'm sorry, Bonnie."

"For what?"

"You know what for," Clara replied, shamefaced. "If there was another way, I would pursue it, but... nothin' else works."

Bonnie forced a smile. "I understand, Mama. I don't blame you. You don't have anything to be sorry for."

"I knew that you knew, but I..." Clara trailed off, her face twisting into a mask of bitter regret. She quickly turned away, her voice thick as she added, "You should go to bed. You've had a long day."

Bonnie nodded. "Goodnight, Mama." She stooped to kiss her mother's cheek. "You're doing the best that you can. Please, know that. Alice and I are... happy, in our own way, and we owe that to you. Alice is happy, at least, and I am content."

"You are?" Clara swallowed.

"I am."

Clara drew in a shaky breath. "And William? Has he written recently? Are his feelings what they were?"

"I believe so," Bonnie told her, "unless he is an exceptionally good liar. Then again, if his feelings had changed, I imagine he would cease writing to me. As he has not, I shall take that as a fortunate sign."

Clara nodded slowly. "That is fortunate indeed." She paused. "When he asks you to marry him, you must say yes. You must let him take you out of here. You mustn't worry for me or Alice, no matter our situation—we will be content. Promise me you will think of your own happiness when he asks you."

"I will think of my happiness, and what it means for all of us," was all Bonnie could promise, certain that William had meant what he said when he assured her that he would save them all. "Perhaps, by then, you and Alice *will* be happy here. If not, you'll come with me. It's that simple, and I won't hear anything to the contrary."

Clara mustered a tight chuckle. "Very well. Now, off to bed with you."

"Yes, Mama." Bonnie kissed her mother's soft, woodsmoke-scented hair and put her arms around her mother's neck for a moment, embracing her. She waited until she felt her mother's hand upon her forearm, returning the affection.

A few moments later, Bonnie retreated from the cupboard under the stairs, and heard the rickety door close as she made her way towards the kitchen to say "goodnight" to Alice.

"I thought I'd stay here for a while," Alice said, as Bonnie appeared in the doorway.

Bonnie nodded in understanding. "Don't stay up too late. I'm going to the steelworks. I should be home before you leave for school."

"The steelworks?" Alice's eyebrows rose up in consternation. "At such an hour?"

Bonnie shrugged. "I won't sleep tonight, but there is always work to be done there; I ought to make myself useful instead of disturbing you and the cousins. It'll keep my thoughts occupied, at the very least."

It was Alice's turn to nod in understanding. "He's never going to get better, is he?"

"No, dear one, I don't think he is," Bonnie admitted, as much to herself as to her little sister. "But miracles *do* happen. Perhaps, he will be one of the fortunate ones."

She did not believe it for a second, but if she had to lie so that Alice could sleep well and continue to find happiness in their new world, then so be it.

Alice returned her gaze to the glowing embers of the fire. "I wish it was your birthday again."

"As do I," Bonnie replied, moving to embrace her sister and plant a kiss on top of her head. "Make sure you finish all of those barley sugars, and don't sit too close to the fire where the sparks can spit."

Alice leaned back into her sister's hug. "Take one for your travels."

"I will." Bonnie placed one more kiss upon her sister's head, took a barley sugar, and headed out of the house, closing the door quietly behind her.

Once upon a time, the darkened, cramped streets and their shady population of miscreants and ravenous rats would have terrified her, but there was no fear in her wounded heart as she set off towards the smoking stacks of the steelworks.

In that moment, there was no greater danger than the devastating thoughts that threatened to swarm her mind, and no darkness more bleak and impenetrable than her father's fate.

Chapter Eleven

"I thought ye were a high-and-mighty sort of lass when ye walked in here, but I know when I'm wrong. You work hard, lass. I admire that, and you'd best believe it'll take ye far in this place," said Dora Linney: a large, ruddy-faced woman of fifty with arms as thick and muscular as any of the men who came in from the factory.

Perspiring profusely from the efforts of the night, but less burdened than before, Bonnie flashed the older woman a grin. "You wouldn't be the first to underestimate me, Mrs. Linney, and I daresay you won't be the last."

"Ah, ye've spirit too!" Dora cackled. "That'll see ye even further than hard work."

It had just been the two of them since Bonnie wandered in off the street the previous night, close to midnight. She had gone directly to the overseer who, at first, had refused her plea to be put to work.

"All we've got is work on the grinders and rollers, and I ain't puttin' ye there," he had said, observing her with a familiarity that had rankled her. *"Wouldn't want ye gettin' a burn or a bit of filin' where it oughtn't be, now, would we?"*

In the end, with sheer stubbornness, she had managed to convince him to find alternative work for her. He had brought her to the steelworks' kitchens, where huge vats of stews and broths and endless trays of bread needed preparing for the end of the night shift and for luncheon and dinner the next day. All workers were entitled to one meal and, for many, it was the only meal they were likely to get.

Bonnie sank down onto a wooden chair, the varnish peeling. "I could fix these," she said, eyeing the worn surface, running her fingertips along it. "My ma and my aunt—all of us, in truth—we do some polishing. We're good at it, too."

"It's a fine thought, but there's no coin for that, lass. We'll keep them chairs 'til they break. Ain't no folks worryin' about gettin' a splinter or two in their backside," Dora replied with a laugh, ladling out a bowl of the hearty meat stew they'd spent all night cooking. What the meat was, was anyone's guess, but Bonnie had learned in her brief time in Sheffield that it was better not to be curious about such things.

The older woman passed the bowl of stew to Bonnie, and dragged over another chair so they could eat their breakfast together. Outside the steam-fogged and smoke-blackened windows, dawn was just beginning to thin out the inky black of the night's sky.

"Mind if I ask what brought ye in tonight?" Dora asked, chewing on a mouthful of bread as she ripped up a roll of bread and handed half to Bonnie.

Bonnie shrugged. "Does it matter?"

"Not a bit, but... ye seem a sweet lass, and usually it's sweet lasses who've found themselves in an unfortunate situation who seek out work at night when it ain't their ordinary shift," Dora replied. "Is yer husband knockin' ye about? Lord knows I shouldn't pry, but I can do a fair bit of knockin' around meself, and I've given a warnin' or ten in my time."

Bonnie stared at Dora. "I'm... not married."

"Yer father, then?"

Bonnie shook her head. "No one is "knocking me around," though I thank you for your concern. My father is sick, and he was... particularly unwell last night. I'm hoping to buy some medicines for him, and for medicine you need money—that's why I came in last night." It was not the whole truth, but she was too tired from stirring and kneading and chopping and washing and carrying huge pots to tell the full story. Nevertheless, she was strangely charmed by Dora's offer to give a warning to anyone who might be hurting her. It was the kindness of the Sheffield people—something she was still not used to.

Dora seemed relieved. "I'm surprised you ain't married: a pretty lass like you."

"I have a... betrothed of sorts, but we're not married yet," Bonnie said, blushing slightly as she ate her stew.

Dora clapped a hand against Bonnie's shoulder. "I knew there'd be a lad somewhere! Ah, well, he better hurry himself along before some other decent lad decides to sweep ye off yer feet."

"He wants to improve his situation first," Bonnie explained, pocketing the bread to give to Alice before she went to school. "He's a tailor. A very fine one at that. That's how we met." Caught up in a wave of sudden, aching affection that staved off her weariness, Bonnie told Dora a selective version of the events that had brought her to Sheffield. "By the beginning of next year, I expect there'll be a wedding. I hope so, anyway," she concluded, her heart full as she thought of William and his parting kiss.

Dora sighed. "Oh, to be young and in love again. Naught like it in this world." She paused. "But you just be careful of men's promises, eh? If he's a good lad, he'll hold true to his word. I hope he *is* that sort of lad."

"He is," Bonnie said, with every confidence. She could not, and would not, believe that William might let her down again, for his promise of love and marriage was like the bell at the end of a shift. It was what she was waiting patiently for, knowing it would improve the situation of everyone around her.

Dora smiled. "I'll keep ye in me prayers, lass, and if ye find yerself wantin' to come and help me in these here kitchens again, ye're more than welcome. Ye're better company and a harder worker than the lass who used to toil with me. She'd sit in that corner over yonder, complainin' of all sorts of aches and pains—different every night, mind ye—and by the time mornin' came, she hadn't lifted a finger."

"I'd like to come back," Bonnie insisted, "but I don't know that I could manage it, with my other position starting at noon. If I think I can, I'll let Mr. Prenton know."

Dora finished what was in her bowl and set it down with a satisfied sigh, patting her rounded belly. "Either way, ye're welcome any time." She glanced at the clock on the wall. "Goodness, ye'd best be gettin' yerself home for a kip if ye're back here at noon. Oh, and make sure Mr. Prenton pays ye for last night's work—he's a scoundrel, him. Will try and rob ye of what's owed if he thinks he can."

"I'll make sure," Bonnie promised, rising on weary feet to collect her cloak and head back out into the cold morning air. "It was a pleasure, Mrs. Linney."

Dora batted a dismissive hand. "Don't you be callin' me Mrs. Linney. We're friends, now, so call me Dora."

"Thank you, Dora." Bonnie smiled, wishing she could explain just how grateful she was to the older woman for keeping her distracted through the night with her endless knowledge of the town, her equally endless stream of gossip about everyone *in* the town, her bawdy jokes, and her frankly heavenly singing voice.

Dora nodded, leaning back in the chair and closing her eyes. "Just remember, if anyone ever gives ye any trouble, ye tell 'em ye're acquainted with me and they'll be gettin' a smack if they so much as say a rude word in yer direction."

"I'll tell them," Bonnie replied, chuckling as she left the unbearable warmth of the kitchens and stepped out into a blast of icy wind, carrying the fire and brimstone scent of the steelworks. For a moment, she thought about retreating back inside and finding a corner to sleep in, but she remembered the half a bread roll in her pocket and pressed on towards home. Alice would be waiting.

***

Following her usual path toward the terraced house in Neepsend, Bonnie had not gone far from the steelworks when she found herself joining a throng of people, flowing in the same direction. It was still dawn, the streetlamps still aglow, and though she had expected to encounter a few people on their way to work, the extent of the crowd was jarring.

"It's washed it all away—that's what I heard," someone said nearby, bringing Bonnie to a halt.

"Naught left, apparently," said another.

"Terrible, int it? But I said to my Phillip when they were buildin' them terraces and cottages that it weren't a good idea to build anythin' so close to the river," a third boasted. "It's them up at Loxley and Malin Bridge I feel sorry for. Wouldn't have known it was comin' 'til it was too late, all of 'em asleep in their beds."

"Same for them in Neepsend," protested a gruff man, limping along on a crutch. "When a dam breaks like that, a messenger on a Derby horse couldn't get word to folk quick enough. Might've been us if the river had chosen a different course."

Bonnie hurried toward the gossipers, grabbing one of them by the arm. "Did you mention Neepsend? Has something happened?"

"Have ye been hidin' under a rock, lass?" the boastful woman retorted.

The man with the crutch intervened, explaining, "The dam up at Dale Dyke went and broke in the night. A big flood came rushin' down through the valleys, washin' away everythin' in its path. With water, ye see, it takes the easiest path—with Neepsend where it is, it was right in the way of the flood."

"You're... certain?" Bonnie choked, her eyes wide.

The man seemed to realise her panic. "Do ye have family there, lass?"

"Everyone," Bonnie gasped, her grip tightening on the arm of the stranger she had grabbed before.

The boastful woman suddenly looked shamefaced. "Well, if they'd any sense, they'll be well enough. It's the villages in the valleys that took the brunt of it."

"I don't reckon ye'll be able to get there," the man on the crutch said more softly, taking hold of Bonnie's free hand. "There are constables, they're turnin' everyone away. I'm sorry to say it, lass, but from what I've heard—there's naught left of Neepsend but bricks. Ye ought to find somewhere to stay until the water recedes. Might be that yer family find ye before ye find them. So long as they weren't right by the river, they'll have got themselves out."

Bonnie stared at him. A second later, she yanked her hand out of his, released her grip on the other stranger, and took off down the street, running as fast as her trembling legs and the crush of the crowd would let her.

Before long, she reached the outskirts of Neepsend... or where it should have been. The terraced houses and ramshackle cottages were all but gone, torn away by the violent fury of the flood; the water levels still higher than they should have been, entirely concealing the houses that had made the mistake of being too close to the river. Her aunt's house was somewhere underneath the churning water, where the bodies of people and livestock floated alongside felled trees and chunks of what appeared to be metal, though it was hard to see in the low light.

All she knew for certain was that her aunt's house was submerged; her home was gone, and it seemed unlikely, even if she had been standing there in broad daylight, that anyone had escaped in time. Not so close to the river, just as the man with the crutch had said.

Numb from head to toe, Bonnie absently put her hand into her pocket, closing her fist around the half a bread roll, crushing it until it was nothing but crumbs.

Chapter Twelve

On a grey morning, the church chiming ten bells to the soft patter of drizzling rainfall, Bonnie found herself on the precipice of a gaping mouth, yawning out of the ground. She was alone, mouthing a silent prayer for the souls who lay buried below, devoid of dignity, their bodies crammed together. It seemed to her that the working class would always suffer that fate— forced to fit wherever there was room, as cheaply as possible. How else could something as awful as a pauper's grave exist? All she had to do was glance toward the main cemetery, glinting with marble headstones and proud mausoleums, to feel the great divide between the poor and the wealthy, even in death.

"They're bringin' more bodies up, lass," a man said, approaching cautiously with a shovel balanced over his shoulder. "Ye might want to make yerself scarce."

Bonnie looked at him and turned away, saying nothing. She doubted he would have understood why she wanted to stand there in prayer, even though layers of soil had already been poured to cover the family she had lost. What *she* could not understand, however, was why she was alone. Where were the other families? Where were the other mourners? Perhaps, they were mourning in their own way, somewhere else. Perhaps, there was no one left in those families to stand at the communal graveside and weep.

"Goodbye, Papa," she whispered, heart breaking. "I hope... there is peace for you, at last. I hope... you can make beautiful dresses again and look down upon us, knowing how loved you were."

Head down, chin pressed to her chest, she walked away from the churchyard and made her slow way back to what remained of Neepsend. All the while, she prayed for the lost souls she would never see again: a tragedy beyond measure. A tragedy she did not think she would ever be able to fathom. Her papa, her cousins, her aunt and uncle. Almost her whole family, lost in one fateful night.

And yet, I am deemed lucky for living. I am deemed lucky for being elsewhere, she mused bitterly, shivering against the cold gusts of wind that cut through the town of Sheffield like a wave of ice-tipped arrows, nipping at her cheeks.

Since the night of the flood, she had barely shed a tear. It was strange to her, for she could feel the tears swelling inside her, and with every reminder and memory of that night, more grief was tipped on top of the last batch, until her heart felt like it might explode from the pressure. Yet, she could not cry, spilling only a tear or two when she knew she ought to be sobbing until there was nothing left.

Because I know there will be greater pain to come, she considered, as the wreckage of Neepsend came into view.

***

Bonnie ducked inside the one-room cottage that she had claimed in the ensuing chaos of the flood. Other families had tried to seize it for themselves, but she had fought tooth and nail, swinging the broken end of a broom like a madwoman, until they backed off. Even that seemed ridiculous to Bonnie; sane, formerly respectable members of society scrapping over the husk of a cottage with its front façade half torn away, its windows and doors gone, its roof partially missing, its floor still wet with floodwater and everything it had brought with it.

A fire crackled in the centre of what had once been the kitchen. Alice stood over it, stirring a pot of something. In the far corner, on a raised platform of crates that Bonnie had picked from the devastation with her bare hands, lay their mother. On a second platform, Annabelle rocked her youngest brother, Christopher—now, her only brother—to sleep as he mewled for milk that would not come.

"It is done," Bonnie said, eyeing the dismal scene with a heavy heart. "I said a prayer for them all."

Annabelle did not look up, her vacant gaze fixed upon her brother.

"Did you lay the flowers I picked?" Alice asked, her lip trembling.

Bonnie nodded, unwilling to say anything more about the awful waste of life and indignity that she had just witnessed. "I'm away to the steelworks at two o'clock," she said instead. "I thought I'd try and sleep first, and if there's a bowl of that soup going spare, I wouldn't mind a sip of it."

"You're going to the steelworks today?" Alice's eyes widened. "But... they said you did not have to return until next week, did they not?"

It had been three days since the flood, and though the owners of the steelworks had been generous, offering those affected a week to find new lodgings and to pay their respects to those who had been lost, Bonnie could not bear another day amongst the suffocating sadness that rose like the floodwaters within the miserable cottage.

Bonnie put on a smile. "We need medicine and nourishment, Alice," she said gently. "Mama must have something for the pain, and the steelworks cannot offer that. But I can earn enough coin for both, for all of us, so that none of you need worry."

"Do not... concern yourself with... me," Bonnie's mother coughed from the makeshift cot, struggling to sit up.

Bonnie went to her, urging her to lie back down. "You took care of us for so many years, Mama. Now, it's my turn."

Bonnie could not look at the mess that a chunk of stone had made of her mother's legs. It did not take a physician to know that they were broken, and though Bonnie had done her best, with her very limited knowledge, to try and set them, she was entirely aware that her mother would never walk again. All Bonnie could do was ease her agony and hope that, when the bones mended—however they mended—Clara would not be in too much pain anymore.

"I thought I'd ask if there's anyone who might agree to feed Christopher, too," Bonnie added, glancing at her cousin, red-faced in the arms of his big sister. "Alice, you ought to make enquiries too. It'll be easier if there's someone nearby."

Alice nodded, pouring out bowls of the thin soup she had been stirring. "I'll ask everyone I can," she promised, passing out the bowls.

Annabelle immediately set hers down on the crates, continuing her vacant-eyed rocking as Christopher's mewling became a shrill cry that pierced the back of Bonnie's skull. Meanwhile, Bonnie set her own bowl down so she could help to lift her mother. Alice raised the bowl of soup to her mother's lips, the sisters working together, conscious of their mother having her fill before they even thought of taking some for themselves.

"Have you... written to... William?" Clara asked, as she finished her last mouthful of soup.

Bonnie froze. "Not yet."

"You should," her mother insisted. "He'll want... to know, if he hasn't... heard already. There might be... somethin' he can do to help... us."

Bonnie nodded slowly. "I'll write to him as soon as I can."

She did not have the strength to tell her mother that she had nothing to write with, as ink and paper were a luxury they could no longer afford. Nor did they have any sort of address that William would be able to reply to; Bonnie did not even know the name of the street where they were surviving, or if the cottage would still be theirs in a week's time. As desperation increased, there was every chance that they would be turfed out. Either that, or when the landlord discovered there were people living in his property without paying a single ha'penny for it. It would not matter to a landlord if most of the cottage was missing.

So, Bonnie sat on the edge of the makeshift cot and sipped her soup, staring out of the rectangle where the door used to be, watching the desolate displaced of Neepsend wandering through the destruction, searching for loved ones, looting for valuables, trying to make sense of what had happened.

***

That night, as Bonnie's shift on the assembly line came to an end, she had her cloak pinned at her throat, ready to leave, when a thought came to her. Hesitating at the door, she turned back, raising her hand to attract Mr. Prenton's attention. He was speaking to the day's overseer, whom he had come to relieve.

"What can I do for you, Miss Acklam?" Mr. Prenton smiled brightly, as if her entire world had not just been swept away for a second time.

Bonnie forced a return smile. "I hoped I might be put to work with Mrs. Linney again tonight. As you might or might not be aware, there was a terrible flood, and it has left my family and I without lodgings. As such, I must endeavour to make as much coin as I can."

"There are easier ways," Mr. Prenton replied, with a nasty gleam in his eyes.

"Be that as it may, I would prefer the difficult way," she replied without pause. "You know that I am an honest and diligent worker and that I cause no trouble. Please, if I may, I would like to take a second shift with Mrs. Linney in the kitchens."

Mr. Prenton sniffed as if he did not like her answer. Then, he shrugged. "If you want to ravage your pretty face by workin' all hours, I won't stop you. I'll put the hours on your pay packet." He paused. "If anyone asks, you're only workin' what you're supposed to."

"Thank you, Mr. Prenton." The weight upon Bonnie's heart lifted ever so slightly, for as long as she could take care of her sister, her mother, and her two remaining cousins, she would have enough purpose to avoid crumbling herself.

Mr. Prenton waved a dismissive hand. "Aye, but if you change your mind about wantin' the easy way, I know a place or two."

"I shan't, but I thank you anyway." Turning on her heel, Bonnie hurried towards the kitchens, hoping she might be able to pocket another bread roll or two for her family.

I can do this, she told herself, suddenly overwhelmed by the prospect of working so many hours, wondering when she would find any time to rest. *I must do this, for we* are *the lucky ones. We are alive, I have employment, and as long as we have that, as long as we have enough, we will rise from this. We will endure.*

After all, she had already been gifted a miracle, when her sister had walked out of the chaos on that terrible morning, holding baby

Christopher in her arms with Annabelle limping along at her side, while an unknown man—a man whose name none of them knew, even now—had carried Clara as if she was the most precious cargo.

We will endure, as we have already done. We will build ourselves another miracle, even if it is the harder path, Bonnie told herself, more insistently.

It was the tiniest flame of hope, and only she could keep it burning. She had not been able to save her father's shop or his business, just as she had not been able to save her father, but she *would* save those who were left.

She would not fail again. And as she thought of what lay before her, she finally allowed the tears to come, her grief pouring out of her in hot streams that stung her scraped and scratched cheeks; injuries from the accidental mudlarking she had performed since the flood.

"I'll keep them safe, Papa," she whispered, clasping a hand to her heart. "I'll keep them safe, and when we have some spare coin, I'll buy you a headstone. I'll buy one for Aunt Katie and the cousins, too—a place where we can go to remember you all."

Somehow, she would create a legacy for those who were gone, even if she had to work her fingers to the bone.

Chapter Thirteen

Sheffield, November 1864

If anyone had asked Bonnie how she had managed to stay alive, and keep her mother, sister, and two cousins alive too, she would not have been able to give an answer. Yet, if she gave herself a moment to think about her aching bones, protesting muscles, arthritic hands, and the thinness of her figure, her clothes hanging off her, it became less of a mystery.

"Ye're not stirrin' another morsel of that stew 'til ye've had a bowl for yerself," Dora demanded, as the church bells in the distance chimed four o'clock in the morning. "And ye're to have a roll of bread an' all. Ye're not to pocket it, else I'll check yer pockets before ye leave and make ye eat it."

Bonnie had not even realised she was stirring the vast vat of meaty stew, for it had become so familiar to her that she could do it in her sleep. Once or twice, she had, almost fallen into the bubbling concoction, saved by Dora's strong grip on the tight knot of Bonnie's apron.

"Can I pocket one, too?" Bonnie asked with a tired smile, stepping down off the footstool that nudged against the vat.

Dora chuckled. "I won't tell if ye won't. Just as long as ye do eat one for yerself."

"I will. It's not that I don't want to—I keep forgetting, that's all," Bonnie tried to explain, sinking down into one of the nearby chairs.

Dora brought over a bowl of stew and one of the biggest rolls, warm from the oven. She sat in the chair next to Bonnie, huffing out a great sigh as she settled herself and passed the bowl and bread to Bonnie.

"How's the wain?" Dora asked, as the two women began eating.

Bonnie shrugged. "Eating us out of house and home. I've never seen such a huge appetite in one so small."

"It's a good sign," Dora said. "Means he'll be a healthy man when he's older—someone to take care of ye all, once he's old enough to start workin'."

"I know it sounds peculiar," Bonnie murmured, between mouthfuls, "but I think he was saved from the flood for a reason. I think he was saved from the flood to save *us*, in a way. We'd have all been miserable without him smiling and laughing and saying his first words and stumbling through the cottage like a drunkard. There was a time when I thought Annabelle would never smile again, or that she'd turn to madness like my father did, but Christopher... he's a piece of magic, I'm telling you. He's brought such joy to that cottage."

Dora nodded. "That's children for ye. They don't know a bad thing has happened when they're that young. So, they help ye forget the bad thing. Where there are children, there's hope." She paused. "What about that William of yers? I've not heard ye speak of him in months, but I'm fair certain ye said ye were to be wed to him this winter, startin' on havin' a gaggle of wains of yer own."

"I wrote but... he never wrote back," Bonnie admitted, swallowing a chunk of bread that lodged in her throat, blocked by the lump that formed whenever she thought of William.

She had written to him every week since the flood, spending coin she did not have on paper and ink and postage stamps. But as the weeks had gone by and no reply had come, she had given up on the endeavour. Either his letters were getting lost due to the lack of proper address on her side or hers had been lost, or he had simply realised that pulling her out of her situation would now be too much, for she would not have been able to leave Annabelle and Christopher behind.

Dora pulled a face. "I hoped that wouldn't happen to ye, but there'll be plenty of fine lads linin' up to propose; I'm certain of it. As long as it int Mr. Prenton, I'll approve."

"Good Lord, no!" Bonnie blurted out, the two women descending into laughter as they exchanged a mutual look of disgust.

It felt good to laugh, and through the long nights at Dora's side, Bonnie was perpetually surprised to find herself chuckling and smiling and gossiping as though she did not have a care in the world. In truth, just as Christopher's joyfulness had brought life and cheer back to the cottage, Dora was responsible for saving Bonnie's sanity. Dora never asked too much of Bonnie, and on the nights when Bonnie was especially exhausted after a long shift at the assembly line, Dora would make her curl up in the corner of the kitchens, underneath a workbench, and tuck her in like she was still an infant, letting her sleep until the end of the night shift sometimes.

"Can you imagine?" Bonnie wiped her eyes, her stomach aching with the laughter.

Dora turned up her nose. "I'd rather not, else I won't eat me stew." She flashed a grin. "Now, what are ye thinkin' for yer birthday? I don't want to impose meself on ye, but there's plenty room at mine if ye want feedin' and some merrymakin'. I always have me house open to dear friends, and ye'd be more than welcome to celebrate there. All of ye."

"I hadn't even thought about my birthday," Bonnie admitted, staring up at the steamed windows of the kitchens. She was somewhat surprised that Dora had even remembered it. "I thought I might snare some rabbits, cook them up for a feast. Maybe buy a cake if I have enough coin."

Dora shook her head. "Ye won't be buyin' a cake, lass. I'll bake ye one, so long as we keep it between us. It can go right in with the bread rolls and ye can sneak it out—no one will be any the wiser."

"I can't ask you to do that," Bonnie protested, forever warmed by the generosity of her dear friend.

"Ye don't need to ask; I'm offerin'. And heaven knows ye need some sweetness in yer life, Bonnie," Dora said. "If ye won't accept for yerself, then accept for yer ma and yer sister and yer cousins. I know that little lad would love a bite of cake, no matter the occasion."

Bonnie could not help but smile. "Thank you, Dora."

"No thanks needed." Dora puffed out her ample bosom, clearly satisfied. "How is yer ma, anyway? Ye said she was standin' up on her own t'other day. She gettin' some strength back in her legs?"

Bonnie nodded. "One is useless, but the other is holding her up. With the crutch I carved her, she's able to move around, though I think it pains her. She won't say, of course—she's as stubborn as you and me—but she's ploughing through her laudanum faster than she ought to be."

"Nasty stuff," Dora remarked. "Expensive, too."

Bonnie chuckled wryly. "I'm very aware of the cost, but if it helps her, I have to keep buying it. I never understood why she gave it to my father when he was at his worst, but now I do. Sometimes, a person will do anything, take anything, just to get a few hours of undisturbed sleep." She paused. "If it didn't have such an awful smell, I'd be tempted to have a drop or two myself."

"Don't ye dare!" Dora chided. "Ye know ye can always sleep here, whenever ye need. I only keep ye with me because I like the company, but I can do it all by meself if all ye ever want to do is sleep."

Bonnie smiled. "I know. You're like machinery. But I like the company almost as much as I like the idea of sleep. You've kept my spirits high throughout this... difficult year, Dora, and I don't know that I'll ever be able to repay you for that kindness."

"Nonsense. Ye don't need to repay a thing. Ye're like me own kin, Bonnie, and ye will be, even if yer tailor from York finally decides to come and keep his promise," Dora insisted, warming Bonnie's soul far more than the stew ever could. "And I meant what I said about yer birthday. Me door will be open if ye need it."

"I won't forget," Bonnie promised, though she hoped that, with a few days to plan something, she would be able to create some cheer in the cottage that would chase away the stark absence of so many loved ones. It would not be her day, but a day for all of them, to find celebration in what they had survived and achieved together.

***

"Why can't we just *buy* rabbits?" Alice complained the following night, as the three young ladies trudged through the moorland beyond the town limits in search of snaring spots. It was something they did often when they were starving and in immediate need of meat, but that did not mean they were all eager to partake.

The moorlands still bore the scars of the flood that had snatched away so much from so many: great trees rotting on their sides, their roots lost with no soil to anchor themselves; boulders sitting in fields where they had no right to be; fragments of masonry and homes that prodded up through the dirt and grass, as if to remind anyone stepping too close of what they used to be, though no one would ever be able to put them back together again.

Still, as nature often did, it had begun to make the devastation and detritus its own; moss grew on the stones and bricks, the dying trees fed myriad creatures and became a new home for animals that might once have feared the high climb, and the sheep and cows grazed as they always had, forgetting that their herds had been thinned alongside those of the humans who owned them.

Annabelle chuckled. "I don't know why ye insist on comin' with us if ye hate it so much. Ye could've stayed with Aunt Clara and the little lamb; we wouldn't have minded, and nor would they."

"I don't hate it," Alice protested, "I just don't understand why we can't buy what we need."

Annabelle glanced at Bonnie, exchanging a knowing look. Although Alice had come to terms with the monumental twists of fate that had changed their lives twice over, she still had not quite relinquished the habits and comforts that she had been accustomed to in York. There were aspects of an existence based on pure survival that still confused her; namely, how thinly they had to spread Bonnie's dual income in order to keep any food on the table.

"Next year, we might be able to," Annabelle said proudly.

Bonnie put an arm around her cousin, hugging her into her side. "It'll be strange without you in the cottage, but I couldn't be happier for you. This is the start of a new future for you, Anna, and I know you're going to do so very, very well there."

"It's only because ye kept us clean and clothed and fed and forced us to stay in our schoolin', Bonnie," Annabelle insisted. "If I'd gone to that house lookin' like a beggar, they'd have laughed in me face or shooed me out. But ye scrubbed me and darned me clothes and taught me what to say—I know that's the only reason they gave me employ."

Bonnie shook her head. "It's because you are who you are. *You* charmed them, and it had very little to do with you being scrubbed and neat."

"I'm going to miss you," Alice mumbled miserably, for Annabelle had become like an additional sister to the mismatched family, and when she went off to begin her employment as a scullery maid at one of the grand houses on the other side of Sheffield, her absence would be keenly felt by everyone.

Annabelle smacked Alice in the arm. "I'll be back every Sunday, and by this time next year, ye'll be workin' alongside me. I'm goin' to talk about ye so often that they'll give ye employment just to shut me up."

"Do you really think they would accept me?" Alice's eyes widened with hope, while Bonnie's heart broke a little more. Of course, Bonnie wanted a secure future for her sister, but the thought of another one of her diminished family leaving the nest was a hard prospect to swallow.

Annabelle nodded confidently. "I know they will. Ye're prettier, ye speak nice, and ye're far cleverer than I'll ever be. Wouldn't be surprised if they start ye as a housemaid, considerin' all that."

"Ladies, I hate to disrupt this conversation," Bonnie said, "but we must be quiet, or we'll scare all the rabbits away and we won't have anything to eat for this birthday of mine except cake."

Annabelle arched an eyebrow. "And that would be a bad thing?"

"It would when your stomach starts hurting from eating only sugar and butter," Bonnie pointed out, smiling.

Annabelle shrugged. "Doesn't sound terrible to me."

As the chattering of the two younger girls settled into companionable silence, the trio stalked through the damp moorland, searching for places to set their snares. Indeed, the entire art of snaring rabbits was something that Annabelle had taught them: an education that might once have made Bonnie wrinkle her nose in distaste but had become a salvation on many occasions since the flood.

I doubt I would recognise the woman I used to be, Bonnie mused, as they found a tangle of gorse bushes, perfect for concealing a snare. *Nor would she recognise me. William likely would not know me now, either.* And though Bonnie often wished that she had not had to lose so much to learn her own strength, she was grateful that, when faced with the insurmountable, she had not yet allowed herself to surrender.

***

"Do you never tire of this?" Alice asked, as the three ladies lay upon a square of oilskin, staring up at the stars. Bonnie had found the oilskin months ago in the wreckage of Neepsend, while the layers of blankets that swaddled the three women against the icy cold were a blessing from Dora.

It was a clear night, and the sky was bejewelled, sparkling like a never-ending reem of silk, embroidered with silver beads: the kind of fabric that their father would have transformed into something just as celestial.

Bonnie turned on her side to look at her sister. "Tire of what?"

"You have but one evening each week where you do not go to work at the steelworks kitchens, yet I have never seen you actually rest upon your day of rest," Alice replied. "Perhaps, a better question would be—aren't you tired?"

Bonnie had to laugh. "I used to be, but I don't feel it anymore."

She could not bring herself to tell the stark truth; that if she allowed herself an evening of rest, doing nothing, it would make her think too much of the past and of their respective futures, and just how long she would have to continue working herself to the bone. A lifetime, no doubt, and that was too crushing to even contemplate.

"I reckon ye'll understand when ye start workin' with me at the Tipton house," Annabelle interjected. "As me ma used to say, "ye don't know ye're born." But that's gettin' older, int it— ye start to understand why yer own ma was always so exhausted, all of the time."

Alice frowned. "Do you miss her?"

Annabelle gave a small shrug. "I would if I didn't have the two of ye and the little lamb and me auntie, but... no, I do miss her, but ye can't miss someone too much else ye'll forget to live, y'know?" She gestured up at the beautiful tapestry of stars. "Anyway, I like to think she's somewhere where she *can* rest. A better place than here."

"I think Papa is too," Alice murmured. "Sometimes, I have these dreams about him, and he's the way he used to be. They're not memories, but... something new, and... I believe he's trying to tell me that he's well, wherever he is in heaven."

Bonnie smiled at the two girls, comforted by the way in which they had both learned to adapt. Indeed, she envied their ability to see hope and optimism, and wished upon the stars above that they would never have any reason to lose that. With any luck, their worst misfortunes were behind them.

"Come, we ought to check the snares," Bonnie said, rising with a groan; her bones chilled by the wintry night.

Annabelle jumped up, helping Alice to her feet, before the two girls rolled up the oilskin and blankets and fastened them to the pack that Bonnie wore for their rabbit-hunting endeavours. After all, poaching and snaring was a necessary crime, and though constables and farmers and landowners alike tended to turn a blind eye, Bonnie was sensible enough not to flaunt their prize of good meat by carrying what they had caught out in the open. It would only take one envious neighbour to blow the whistle, and, at the very least, they would not be able to snare again for months. At the very worst, they would be sentenced for poaching.

In the still silence of the night, with a billion glittering lanterns and a smiling moon to light their way, the three ladies stole across the moorland to see what their snares had managed to capture. Bonnie had a good feeling about it, though she could not explain why. Perhaps, it was because the moon was so cheerful, like it knew there were fair tidings ahead.

"We got one!" Annabelle declared, glancing back at Bonnie and Alice, who trailed behind.

Bonnie froze, her eyes fixed on something much taller and more menacing than a rabbit caught in a snare, emerging from behind a coppice of spiny gorse bushes. Three men, large as giants, coming right at them.

"Run!" Bonnie howled, but it seemed that only the encroaching men heeded her instruction as they broke into a sprint, stampeding toward the three women with their arms outstretched, ready to snare a few pests of their own.

Chapter Fourteen

"Excuse me?" Bonnie called to one of the passing constables, neat and warm in his navy cloak, while she and her wards shivered violently in the holding cell of the local constabulary.

The constable scowled at her. "What?"

"Might we have a blanket or two, so we do not freeze to death whilst we wait?" Bonnie replied, trying her best to sound polite.

The constable rolled his eyes. "I'll see if we've any lyin' around."

He walked off without another word, leaving Bonnie gripping the cold iron bars in desperation. *She* did not care if she froze, but she refused to allow her sister and her cousin to suffer. Indeed, she had already decided that she would take the entire blame for the poaching misdemeanour, no matter what it cost her.

"Why did they take our pack from us?" Alice bemoaned, huddled in the corner next to Annabelle; the two girls sharing one another's heat.

Bonnie shook her head. "To punish us for surviving, of course. Those wretched men knew we had taken nothing from the snares, but how would we learn our lesson if they didn't lie?"

As the two girls went back to their miserable shivering, their faces blanched with the fear of what might happen next, Bonnie held her vigil at the bars, praying that some mercy would come. Even if they had done something criminal, did they not deserve some kindness on so cold a night? It was not as if they had killed anyone or robbed anyone or caused anyone injury, yet they were being treated as if they were the worst possible villains.

Twenty minutes—and no blankets—later, another constable walked past the holding cell with his cloak in his hands, cursing under his breath. A brass button hung loose like a fishhook on a line, and it appeared that the seam of his lapel had torn. Considering the pride that these constables took in their appearance, it seemed to be quite the tragedy.

"Excuse me?" Bonnie called out again, sticking her hand through the bars to touch the man's shoulder as he went by.

The constable jumped, as if he had not seen Bonnie standing there. "What do you want?" he asked sourly.

"I can fix it," she blurted out, fumbling in her dress pocket for the small leather pouch that held her needle and thread—the one thing the constables had not dared to take, considering its location. It was mainly a keepsake, an ageing bone of her past life, but it come in handy countless times since her shamed departure from York.

The constable paused, frowning. "Pardon?"

"Your button and that torn seam—I can fix them," she hurried to reply, opening out the pouch with stiff, shaky fingers. "I was a seamstress. *Am* a seamstress. If you would allow me, I can make it look as good as new again."

For what felt like an eternity, the constable observed her, his gaze flitting up and down the hallway and back to her in quick succession, until she was half dizzy with the movement of his eyes. In truth, she did not know what she hoped to achieve by offering such a generous gift, but her father and mother had always taught her to be kind, for you never know where the ripples of that kindness might take you.

"I suppose there'd be no harm in it," the constable said, at last, warily passing his cloak through the bars of the holding cell. But it seemed he was not done, as he unbuttoned his waistcoat and passed that through, too. "There's a rip in it, close to the pocket, and my watch keeps falling out. You couldn't fix that an' all, could you?"

Bonnie nodded effusively. "Certainly, sir."

"How long will it take you? I can't be walking around the constabulary in a state of undress, else I'll get a reprimand," he muttered, his gaze darting up and down the long, mahogany-wainscoted and dark green hallway once more.

Bonnie assessed the tears with her fingertips, chewing on her lower lip. "Half an hour at most, if you want it to appear as if it was never torn."

"Aye, well, do that. I'll come back in half an hour." The constable moved as if he meant to walk away, only to turn back. "What have they put you in here for? You speak too nice and look too... clean to be a bawd."

Bonnie blinked. "I am no bawd, sir." She sucked in a breath. "My family suffered in the flood, sir. There were twelve of us before it swept our home away, and now there are only the three of us. Annabelle over there; she has an affliction of the lungs from swallowing too much of the water. Alice, the other one, she was partially blinded when a wall caved in on her. As such, I cannot work as much as I need to, and... we were starving, sir. We hoped to snare a few rabbits for a memorial feast, sir, for the birthday of one of us who were lost."

It did not sit well with her to lie about their situation, but it was no less than the truth for so many of the families who had been caught in the Great Sheffield Flood.

And if she could somehow play upon this man's sympathies and manipulate freedom from a few small lies, she knew God would forgive her.

The constable's eyebrows raised up ever so slightly, his expression softening just a touch. "And you were a seamstress before the flood?"

"I was, sir."

He pursed his lips. "Well, I'm… uh… sorry for that. A terrible business." He cleared his throat. "I'll come back in half an hour."

With his head bowed, he strode away, and though her hands were frozen stiff, her fingers aching with the pain of months of stirring pots of stew, filing down cutlery and other such luxuries, and polishing everything to a fine sheen, alongside the toil of keeping a household in order, Bonnie sat down and set to work upon the cloak and waistcoat. There was a soot-stained oil lamp resting upon a nearby stool, offering the only half-decent light to see by, but if she had to strain her eyes to get it done, so be it.

"What are you doing?" Alice asked feebly, hugging her knees to her chest.

Bonnie took a breath. "Saving our skins, I hope."

***

Half an hour later, as promised, the constable returned. He brought a second lantern and two woollen blankets with him, evidently not realising that they might have been more useful before he had made himself scarce.

"Is it done?" the man asked, placing the lantern and the blankets into the holding cell through the bars, where Annabelle grabbed them as if they were bits of gristle being thrown into a pit of ravenous dogs.

Bonnie wearily got to her feet, her neck and back burning with the effort of being hunched over the cloak and waistcoat, painstakingly feeding the needle and thread through the thick material.

There had been one spool left in the leather pouch that had once belonged to her father, rescued quite by accident by Bonnie's mother, who had stowed the pouch away in her apron for safe-keeping; an apron she had been wearing when she escaped the flood.

Now, that spool was all but used up and she doubted she would have enough coin for a new one.

"It is done," she confirmed, giving the constable his clothes back.

The man squinted at the two garments, turning them over in his hands by the light of the lantern, his eyes widening with each passing second as he no doubt realised he could no longer tell where the tear in the seam and the rip by the pocket had been.

It was not an easy technique, and not one she had done before, but she had watched her father enough times. As it turned out, she had not forgotten everything of her former life, but whether or not her past would save her present and her future remained to be seen.

"It's a pity your sisters aren't well," he said, after a moment. "You're a gifted seamstress, and no mistake. I'd wager they miss you terribly wherever it was you used to work."

Bonnie dipped her head. "Thank you, sir."

"It's me who ought to be thanking you," the constable replied with a smile.

"You take some refuge under those blankets, and... uh... rest awhile. I'm certain you won't be waiting for much longer."

Bonnie peered up at him. "Will we be taken to prison?"

"I can't say either way," the constable replied, with a note of apology in his voice. "Poaching isn't taken too lightly, which I'm sure you know."

Bonnie nodded solemnly. "I do, sir, and I would not have done it, but my sisters were desperate for something to eat. They had no part in it; I only brought them with me because I can't leave them alone, considering their respective ailments. Even if they had wanted to help me, they would not have been able to, for the same reason."

"Just... get yourself warm, and I thank you again for what you've done. I'd have been in bother if my superiors had seen me with tarnished uniform," the constable said stiffly, before continuing on up the hallway and disappearing into one of the rooms that branched off.

As Bonnie heard the door close, she sank to her knees right there in front of the bars, resting her forehead against the cold iron as her heart dropped into her stomach. It had all been for nothing. Her act of kindness would go unrewarded, and she only had herself to blame. Time and time again, Dora had warned her that constables were not to be trusted, yet Bonnie had put her faith in one, hoping that, somehow, it would save the three of them.

"Are they going to let us go?" Annabelle asked shakily.

Bonnie barely had the strength to answer, tears welling in her eyes as she whispered an exhausted, "I do not know, girls. I do not know."

***

Bonnie did not know how she had managed to fall asleep on bent knees, with her forehead resting against two hard bars, but she knew her body had found a way as the rattle of keys in a lock jolted her from an uneasy slumber. Her eyes shot open, her heart lurching in her chest as she hurried to her feet and staggered back, confused by the scene before her.

The constable with the torn uniform opened the cell door wide, but he was not alone. Another constable, the one who had refused to bring blankets, stood behind him with an expression of dark curiosity upon his grizzled face.

"I've spoken with my superiors," said the first man, "and there's been an agreement that we ought to let you go. But, before we do, we've to make sure that you understand the importance of what you did wrong. Poaching for any reason is a serious transgression, and if you're caught doing it again, there'll be no leniency for you."

Bonnie nodded in a daze. "I understand, sir."

"Very well. Then, you're all free to leave," the younger, more pleasant constable said, standing aside so the three ladies could depart the draughty, mouldering cell that smelled potently of human fear and despair.

Bonnie rushed to the corner and helped her sister and cousin to get to their feet, letting the blankets fall to the ground as she ushered them out of the cell as quickly as she could. They had heard her previous lies, and though it looked rather ridiculous, Alice made a concerted effort to appear as if she could not see properly, while

Annabelle expelled the most phlegmatic, vulgar cough that Bonnie had ever heard, directing it as close to the constables as she dared.

"Apologies," she mumbled, putting her hand over her mouth. "I can't help when it happens."

Despite herself, Bonnie had to hide her face against Alice's hair to stop the constables from catching the smile that refused to be suppressed.

The three women, arms around each other, were almost at the constabulary door when a hand seized Bonnie by the wrist, yanking her out of the huddle so violently that she almost lost her footing. As she had been the central pillar holding up her sister and cousin, they, too, were nearly sent flying by the sudden jolt.

"You know you got lucky then, don't you?" The constable who had refused to bring blankets glared at Bonnie as if she had personally offended him.

Bonnie put on her best expression of apology, though she felt not a lick of guilt for trying to feed her family. "I promise you, as I have promised your associate, that I have no intention of committing such a wretched act again."

"If you do, there'll be no mercy," the constable shot back.

Bonnie met his gaze with a quiet defiance, imagining him as a medieval torturer who relished his work. "I understand, sir." She paused, curving her lips into a smile. "Now, if you please, I should like to get my sisters home so they can rest beside the fire. Might I have the pack that you took from me when we entered?"

"I don't know nothin' about no pack," the constable replied, smirking.

Bonnie shrugged. "No matter. Good evening to you, sir."

Frustrated by the loss of the pack but unwilling to give the constable even a hint of satisfaction at seeing her plead for it, she led her sister and her cousin straight out of the constabulary without looking back. Free or not, the night's arrest had been a painfully close shave, and not one that Bonnie was prepared to repeat for the sake of a few rabbits to eat in honour of a birthday she did not care about.

I must swallow my pride, she knew, her heart heavy. For months, even during the most desperate days, Bonnie had refused to surrender her dignity and go to one of the nearby churches to beg for food. She did not know why, in truth, but she suspected it had something to do with her old life, and the money her family had given to the York Minster to help the needy.

Despite their situation, she supposed she had refused to be considered one of the needy and, thus far, she had managed to scrimp and scrape and scrabble for enough food and coin to keep herself from joining one of those long, sad lines for soup and bread.

Of course, she knew she could go to Dora's lodgings, taking her dear friend up on her kindly offer, but that would have meant leaving Bonnie's mother behind at the cottage, alone.

There was no way that Bonnie's mother could walk to Dora's lodgings, nor could any of them carry her so far, and Bonnie would not, under any circumstances, leave her mother by herself on the first anniversary of the day their lives changed forever, and the first birthday celebrated since her husband and her sister and most of her nieces and nephews had been lost to the flood.

"Let us go home," Bonnie said softly, as a cold blast of winter air struck her feverish cheeks. Overhead, the night sky had been watered down to an inky blue, like navy paint dropped into a glass of water. Soon, it would be dawn, and if Bonnie was fortunate, she might be able to steal a few hours of sleep before the steelworks called once more and she would have to drag her aching, exhausted body to the assembly line, for employment and money did not care if she was tired to the point of delirium.

***

The sun was still hesitating to emerge from the horizon as Bonnie, Alice, and Annabelle reached the dilapidated cottage on the edge of Neepsend. However, there were lanterns burning behind the squares of patchwork material that were stretched across the empty windows, their glass smashed by the force of the water.

Bonnie stared at the silhouetted lanterns, a cold prickle beetling down the back of her neck. Her mother knew better than to keep the oil burning when it cost so much; not to mention, her mother had been fast asleep with Christopher when the three women departed for the moorlands.

"Mama?" Bonnie hurtled through the makeshift door, cobbled together from planks of wood she had found in the debris.

Her mother sat by a roaring fire, stuffed with expensive coal, cradling Christopher in her arms. She looked up as Bonnie approached, and there were haunting tears in her red-rimmed eyes, her bottom lip trembling as she struggled to find her voice.

"I... don't know what's wrong with him," Clara managed to choke out. "He... awoke screamin' and... his face was so red and so hot. I gave him... some of my... laudanum and... he hasn't moved since. He's... breathin', but it's so... faint and... I don't know what to do. I can't call upon a physician as I might've done once. I've just been... sittin' here, prayin' for the best, but... he's so pale and hot, Bonnie. I don't know what to do."

Bonnie stared in disbelief at her mother. "You gave him laudanum?"

"The tiniest bit," her mother replied, her breath catching. "I... thought it... would help."

Bonnie reached for the boy, pulling him into her arms. Behind her, Annabelle tried to take the child from Bonnie, but Bonnie held him tighter.

"Let me have him," Annabelle urged, her eyes wide with fear. "If he's goin' to die, he's not dyin' in no-one's arms but mine."

Bonnie held her nerve, realising that she truly had become a sort of mother to them all. "He's not going to die," she promised, sounding more confident than she felt. "I have some coin—not much, and it was supposed to pay for you and Alice to buy a few things before you left, but it'll be enough to get him seen by a physician."

If not, I know where I can get some more coin quickly, she neglected to add, for it would have broken her heart, her mother's heart, and her sister's heart in one fell swoop.

"Stay here," Bonnie continued at a clip. "Warm yourselves from the cold of tonight, then douse that fire and those lanterns, or we'll have naught to see us through the next few days. I'll return as soon as I can."

Annabelle shook her head. "I'm comin' with ye."

"Don't, Anna," Bonnie replied, hardening her voice. "Stay here and ensure that *you* don't fall ill, so you'll be here for the little lamb when he comes home, safe and well."

Tears twinkled in Annabelle's eyes. "If he's goin' to die, he's—"

"I'll bring him to you, without delay," Bonnie promised.

With that, she ran from the cottage with Christopher tight against her chest, pumping her depleted legs as fast as they would go, heading for the only physician she knew of who was close by. The same physician who had prescribed Bonnie's mother with the laudanum she could not resist; the same laudanum that might kill the boy in Bonnie's arms by the time the sun finally decided to rise.

Chapter Fifteen

Bundled up in a threadbare blanket that she had repurposed as a cloak, Bonnie waited in the biting cold, shuffling from foot to foot and blowing into her hands as her eyes flitted up the lengthy line of desperate souls like her, wondering when her turn would come.

She had heard from others in the line—those who were not unaccustomed to the practice of receiving aid—that people could wait through the entirety of the night without ever having a morsel of food, though some people would just keep waiting until the following evening, their bellies incapable of getting any emptier as they stayed in their place.

Apparently, it was not uncommon, especially in the winter, for those who were waiting to die where they stood.

"Lucky we're so close to a graveyard, eh?" one man had joked, though Bonnie saw no reason to find the situation amusing. Then again, she supposed that everyone contended with their misfortune in different ways. She withdrew into herself, others jested until their abject misery no longer seemed so unbearable.

"How's it lookin'?" a young woman, standing behind Bonnie, asked another woman who was passing by on her way out of the church, flanked by four pale and haggard children who clung to her skirts.

The woman with the four children shrugged. "They're thin on soup and there's not a bit of bread left, but it's always the way. Too many mouths need feedin'."

She walked off into the dark with her children in tow, like an eerie entourage, leaving Bonnie with an even more hollow feeling in her stomach. If she could not secure enough food for her family, they would starve. It was not a unique tale.

All she had to do was observe the thin, emaciated bodies ahead of her and behind her, and note the ghoulish, sunken faces and vacant eyes of everyone to know that she was not special.

Since the night of the poaching arrest, and Christopher's unexpected illness, made worse by Clara Acklam's attempt to help him, Bonnie had spent every coin the family possessed to try and make Christopher better.

He had been at the physician's residence for three days, but that night would be his last under the constant care of Doctor Tucker, for though the physician was kindly enough, there was nothing more in her coffers to offer and Doctor Tucker was not the sort of man who gave his services charitably.

I must hope I have done enough to save him. I must pray that it was worth it, and where better to pray than here, Bonnie told herself, wishing that the steelworks could have been open on the one night where she needed it the most. But, being Saturday, it would not open its doors again until the day after tomorrow and had closed its doors at noon that day due to a broken furnace, robbing Bonnie of two desperately required shifts and the money that came with them.

Just then, a sound drifted out over the shadowed graveyard, weaving down the icy streets of Sheffield, mingling with the rustle of the winter winds that shook the bare branches of the nearby trees. The church choir had begun to sing, rehearsing for evensong. Or, perhaps, it *was* evensong, and more time had passed than Bonnie thought.

As time continued to bend and stretch around her, making hours feel like days and minutes resemble eternities, Bonnie shuffled diligently forward until, at long last, she found herself at the entrance to the church. A stained-glass Virgin Mary stared down at her with sorrowful eyes, a spatter of rainfall landing upon her cheek, the droplets rolling down her face like tears for the poor souls who sought benevolence in her house of worship.

On shaky legs, for she had not eaten more than a bread roll or two since before the snaring incident, choosing to save her portion of stew and bread for her family, Bonnie approached the tables where food was being served.

A stern-faced woman ladled out a bowl of watery soup without so much as a, "Cold night tonight, isn't it?" She pushed the bowl towards Bonnie, grumbling, "You can eat it over there. Put the bowl back when you're done."

"I... need three bowls," Bonnie replied hesitantly. "My family needs them. If at all possible, might I take the bowls and bring them straight back, as soon as my family have eaten?"

The stony-eyed woman looked Bonnie dead in the eyes, showing no shred of pity. "Anyone who wants feeding has to be here. Do you know how often we've heard that story, and it turns out those three bowls are for one person? Or how often those bowls don't come back?"

"Then, might I take this one bowl and bring it back?"

The woman sneered. "You eat it where you're told, or you get nothing." She held out her hand to take the bowl back. "It's your choice, Miss."

"I'll do as I'm told," Bonnie replied sheepishly, already conjuring a plan as to how she might be able to sneak the soup out of the church without arousing suspicion.

Looking as downtrodden and solemn as she could, Bonnie moved to the pews where others like her were devouring their watery soup as if it was a grand feast laid out after a lengthy spell of fasting. She sat down on the very edge of the pew farthest away from the serving tables, curving herself around the bowl of soup that she balanced upon her lap.

Taking her time, she made the motions of someone eating, glancing back at the serving tables every so often to see if the stern woman was watching her.

Certain that she had been forgotten, Bonnie tucked the bowl in the crook of her arm and draped the makeshift cloak over the precious goods, before picking up an empty bowl that had been abandoned on floor. Making a discreet show of wandering back to the serving tables, she put the empty bowl on the wooden surface, passed a grateful nod to the unkind serving lady, and headed out of the church as fast as she could without spilling a drop of the soup.

Keeping her head down, refusing to answer any of the questions that were flung her way from the remaining line of ravenous bodies,

Bonnie was convinced she had made her escape... when she suddenly felt a hand upon her shoulder.

"Excuse me?" a deep, rumbling voice said.

Bonnie froze, for if she tried to break away from the hand resting on her shoulder, she would surely spill too much of the precious soup. So, with a gathering frustration, she slowly turned to face the man who had caught her.

As she looked into the green eyes of the fellow standing before her, noting the way his golden-brown hair shone in the glow of the church-light, his familiar, leonine face easing nervously into a smile, she thought she must have succumbed to the delirium of starvation, at last. William could not possibly be standing there. She was imagining him, seeing whom she longed to see.

"I found you, my love," he said softly, bringing his rough palm to her cheek, the warmth of it taking away the nip of the wind. "I knew I would find you. I never lost hope."

Bonnie blinked. "You... are not real." She brought her hand up to cover his, and though she felt the solidity of his flesh and the heat of his touch, she still could not believe it. "You cannot be real. You... forgot me."

"Never," he replied thickly, tears glittering in his eyes. "I have been searching, my love. For months, I have been searching."

She shook her head. "I told you where I was. You would not have needed months to find me."

"You may have told me, but I did not receive your words," William said, brushing his thumb across the wind-burned apple of her cheek. "Mr. Shannon is precisely the wretch you warned me he was. When news of the flood reached us in York, and I asked if I might journey to Sheffield to find you, he refused. After that, it seems he intercepted the letters that you sent to me, my love, and had them burned so that I might think that you were gone. I only discovered the truth when I found a single piece of a letter in the fireplace of the workshop: it said, "All my love and hope, Bonnie." I confronted Mr. Shannon and he denied it, but I did not believe it, and another apprentice confirmed my suspicions. I left the very same day to come here, looking for you."

Bonnie stared at him, wanting to put her faith in him, but with months of anger and sorrow twisting knots around her lungs, she could not do it. She had changed too much, been disappointed too many times, and had already grieved the loss of the love they had once shared. To hear him say that he had been looking for her was like seeing a man come back to life—too impossible and shocking to comprehend.

"I thought you were dead, my love," William continued, his voice hitching. "I tried not to give up hope, but as the months passed and you could not be found, I feared the worst. But I've been helping here at the church since my arrival in Sheffield, praying that one day you'd appear."

Bonnie narrowed her eyes at him. "How have you survived so many months, as you say you have, without employment? One can't live by helping alone."

"I "inherited" some money on the day I abandoned York and that mockery of a shop," he explained shyly. "There was a bolt of rare silk that had not yet been sold to the mercer, after Mr. Shannon took everything that belonged to your family. He forgot about it, but I did not.

I kept it hidden, and on the day that I left, I took it with me. I sold it for a small fortune, and, with that fortune, I have opened my own tailor's shop in the centre of town, not far from the cathedral. I have watched from my shop windows every day, wishing you would just pass by, praying with all my might that you were alive and well."

Bonnie's breath caught in her throat. "I am alive, at least."

"And everyone else?" he asked warily, taking a half step closer to her, almost upending the soup that still balanced in the crook of her arm.

She swallowed thickly. "Might you walk with me? I... fear I have bent the rules of the church's charity, and if I am found with the contraband, we might both be in trouble." She paused, stroking his hand to try and convince herself he was real. "I will tell you everything as we walk, but not here."

"I will follow you anywhere you wish to lead me, my love," he told her, slipping his hand into hers, and though she still could not believe he was actually there and she was not hallucinating, she did not remove her hand from his as they set off into the darkness together.

***

An hour later, seated upon the low wall outside the steelworks, the chimneys slumbering, the silence deafening, there was nothing that William did not know. Bonnie had informed him of everything that had happened, the good and the terrible, since the Acklam family's arrival in Sheffield. And though she had finished speaking at least five minutes ago, William had still not said a word.

"I should never have allowed you to leave," he murmured, some time later. "I should've asked you to marry me, long before Mr. Shannon came for your father's business. I should've asked you to marry me the night before you left. We'd have found a way to survive. Heaven knows you have the strength of will to survive, after all you've endured. I think I said it once before, but I'll say it again—you're stronger than I ever could've imagined you to be."

Bonnie dipped her chin to her chest, kicking a weed that sprouted from the dirt. "I don't think I could have imagined that such things would befall me, either, nor that I would've been able to live through them."

She paused. "To think that you were here, all this time—I do not know what to make of that. I suppose I have had no need for tailoring, so I had no cause to find one in this town." It was meant in jest, but William looked at her with such anguish that she wished she had held her tongue.

"I'm sorry, Bonnie," he whispered, bringing his hands up to cradle her face. "I am so very sorry that it took me so long. I'm sorrier still that I ever agreed to work for that awful man, Mr. Shannon. I shouldn't have done it. I regretted it as soon as you'd departed, but... I can't undo it now. I can only strive to make things better, now that I've found you."

Bonnie's eyes flew wide, remembering the reason she had gone to the church in the first place. The soup was cold, now, but there were still mouths to feed.

"I must go," she said, jumping to her feet. "I'll come to the church tomorrow to find you. Everyone is waiting for me."

"Let me come with you," William urged, but Bonnie was suddenly ashamed of the ramshackle cottage and the dilapidated district where she lived. It was no place for a well-to-do tailor with his own business. Nor did she want him to worry too much by seeing where she had been residing since the flood; it was one thing to hear an account of it, and quite another to see it firsthand.

Bonnie shook her head. "I will come to the church tomorrow," she repeated. "It is late; we both need to rest. I must be awake at dawn to speak with the physician and collect Christopher, so there is little use in you staying with me now. Tomorrow, dear William. Tomorrow. Please."

If William thought her plea was strangely desperate, he did not say so, nor did he try to persuade her to let him follow. Although, she could feel the hesitancy in him as he stood to bid farewell to her.

"Do you promise you will come to the church?" he asked softly, taking hold of her cold hands. "If you don't, I'll have to search for you, and I will, too. After all, it will be your birthday, and I would not miss it."

She mustered a stiff laugh, her heart full at the knowledge that he had remembered her birthday. "I'll be there, but now, I must be elsewhere."

"I've missed you, Bonnie," William murmured, closing the gap between them, letting one hand fall away from hers to slip around her waist instead, pulling her closer. "You don't know how many nights I've prayed for this—to see you again. It breaks my heart that you ever thought I'd forgotten or forsaken you."

She could not say that she had missed him in return, for it was too small a word for so large a feeling. How could she tell him that she had stood upon the edge of a mass grave and mourned not only the loss of her family but the loss of him?

How could she ever explain that a part of her had died when she had given up on writing to him, knowing he would never write back? How could she put into words how much she loved him still, when her own broken heart had not yet accepted that he had returned for her, just as he had promised?

As with all things, it would take time, and with Christopher still unwell, she did not have the luxury of it. Not yet.

"I must go," she said softly, gazing up into his green eyes; the colour of the weeping willows of York in the summertime.

Before she could take one step to depart, his lips were upon hers, gentle and unsure. A caress of hope between two people who had been separated not only by distance, but by the crevasse of change that yawned between them. A bridge, a promise, a farewell until tomorrow instead of an unknown reunion.

Stunned by the kiss, Bonnie did not respond immediately, but if this *was* a dream, it was the nicest she had had in months, and she was determined not to wake up for a few more moments.

And so, pressing her palms to his sturdy chest, slipping her hands beneath his lapels to steal some of his warmth, she kissed him back with a longing that she had not allowed herself to feel until then.

Perhaps, a kiss was better than words when it came to how much she had missed him.

Still holding onto her, shielding her from the bitter weather with his body, William pulled back slowly. "I mean to keep my promise, Bonnie," he whispered, resting his forehead against hers. "I said I would pledge my love to you this winter, if you'd learned to forgive me. I won't ask now, but... nothing has changed for me, love."

"I know," she replied, taking a deep breath before pressing one last kiss to his lips. "Goodnight, William. Sleep well, and I'll see you tomorrow."

He loosened his grasp of her, and she melted away from the safety of his arms, heading down the steep cobbled road toward the cottage she called home. Every five steps or so, she looked back over her shoulder to make sure he was still there, not a figment of her imagination. And there he stood, his hand raised in a wave, not moving from the spot where they had kissed again at long last until she turned a corner and could no longer see him.

Whipped by the wind that whistled through the town, Bonnie smiled to herself, picturing him waiting there all through the rest of the night and the coming day, so they would never lose one another again.

Chapter Sixteen

But Bonnie did not make it to the church the following day, nor was there anything festive or cheerful to celebrate in the crumbling cottage where piercing screams had replaced any merrymaking and the cake that Dora had made had been eaten in a ravenous hurry, slices cut without ceremony or purpose, purely to fuel the family within through another sleepless, worrisome day.

Christopher had returned from the physician the previous morning, the news dire. Bonnie did not know how she had stood in front of Doctor Tucker without her legs buckling and her grief crushing her, but she had, carrying Christopher back to the cottage like a mean-spirited gift to ruin the faith of her family.

"How is his fever?" Bonnie asked upon waking, the morning after that hopeless, joyless birthday. Although, she did feel about a decade older.

Annabelle sat half-asleep against the rear wall of the cottage, her head lolling as she held her brother in her arms. No one had been able to take the child from his sister since Bonnie had come back from the physician, and though it would have been easy to pluck him from Annabelle's arms right then, no one desired to part them.

Alice sighed. "He isn't howling anymore, but he is still hot to the touch. Won't drink, won't eat."

"He looks redder, too, and his tongue is so swollen," Clara added grimly, stirring the pot over the fire.

Bonnie, who had slept for no more than an hour or two, swung her legs over the side of the cot she shared with Alice and started for the door. "I won't be gone long," she said, stifling a yawn.

"Where are you going?" Alice asked with a pointed look, for she was the only one that Bonnie had told about her encounter with William.

Bonnie shook her head discreetly. "Doctor Tucker said silver nitrate or saltpetre might help him, but I couldn't pay for it then and there," she explained, pausing to take a piece of cake from the plate nearest the door. "I'll see what the dispensary can give me and bring it back before I have to go to the steelworks."

"Shall I come with you?" Alice was already on her feet, but Bonnie shook her head.

"You should stay and help Mama and Annabelle. I can manage." What Bonnie could not admit was that she needed a moment alone to clear her thoughts and figure out what to do about the health of everyone else. After all, Christopher had been diagnosed with scarlet fever, and it did not discriminate; the contagion could easily seize all of them, and she needed to be prepared if it did, stocked with as much silver nitrate as the dispensary would give her in order to counteract the poison of the sickness.

I'm sorry, William, a sad voice whispered in her head, for meeting with him now had become a terrible risk. The miasma that radiated from Christopher might be clinging to her at that very moment, spreading the ailment into her body, and she would not put William in more danger than she already had until she knew she was safe.

***

Tapping her foot impatiently, Bonnie wished she had accepted Alice's request to join her. The morning was stretching ever closer to noon, when she was due at the steelworks for her shift at the assembly and polishing line, and if she was late, she would be forced to face the smug wrath of Mr. Prenton.

He seemed to relish nothing more than to put her in her place, always reminding her that there were easier ways to make coin for her family—a desperate possibility that, until William had reappeared in her life, had begun to seem more like a necessity.

I blame Alice for forgetting that we no longer live a comfortable life, but I have forgotten too, Bonnie lamented, for the only reason she had not permitted Alice to join her was because the dispensary was in a rather shady part of town; the line for free medicines made up of drunkards and degenerates and beggars and impoverished women like herself, who had no other means to acquire the tonics and powders and tinctures and oils that could lessen their suffering.

A charitable endeavour, but a heart-rending one to see with one's own eyes.

In some foolish way, she still wanted to protect Alice from the worst of the world, though they lived amongst poverty every day, and a short walk in any direction from the cottage was a never-ending carousel of misery and sorrow.

A constant display of how low humans could be brought without expiring.

Ahead of her, Bonnie noticed a young woman huddle her two children closer to her, both infants coughing into her skirts, their cheeks as flushed as poor Christopher's.

And as a sharp wind cut down the line, they turned their red faces to the cooling whip of it. There was a storm coming, in more ways than one, and as Bonnie looked up at the sky, where clouds swelled menacingly, she sensed she had more to worry about than making it to the steelworks in time for her shift to begin.

"There's people waitin'! People that's been waitin' hours!" a cry went up from nearby, though the thrum of the wind distorted the origin.

"Get to the back!" another voice barked.

All of a sudden, the line began to writhe and jostle around a small group of men, who were shoving one another with dark vengeance glinting in hollow eyes. Those behind the group pushed back while those in front pushed forward, trying to avoid the flailing limbs and clenched fists as the fight leapt from a quarrel to a full-bodied brawl.

The woman with the two red-faced children seemed unaware of the tussle, perhaps overwhelmed by a feverish delirium herself, while the chaos was getting ever closer to her.

Frightened bodies, seeking an escape, paid no heed to the small children who blocked their path of avoidance, and if that young woman did not come to her senses soon, there was every chance that those poor children would be caught in the tide of trouble, stampeded and stomped on by those who wanted to get away from the fight while holding their place in the line.

Cursing inwardly, Bonnie darted ahead to the young woman and grabbed hold of her hand, attempting to pull her and her children to safety.

But the woman glared at her, wrenching her hand away with a violence that startled Bonnie. A moment later, the woman shoved her, clearly believing that Bonnie was trying to steal her place.

Bonnie might have kept her balance if it had not been for the backwards push of bodies, undulating away from the fight.

A knee caught her in the leg, an elbow jabbing into her side, a foot snagging on the back of hers... and she was falling, with no way to stop herself.

Her back hit the hard pavement with a winding thud, her head dazed as it struck the stone, and all around her, legs staggered backwards, unaware of her presence or not caring that she was there.

Feet kicked her, her helpless body trodden on in desperation, and though she tried to protect herself, rolling onto her side and hugging herself, it was no good. The crowd kept coming, kept moving, oblivious to the fact that they might kill her.

My family needs me, she prayed, screaming it in her mind. *Don't let me die here. Please, God, don't let me die here.*

"Everyone, away with ye!" a loud voice bellowed from far away. "Ye act like animals, ye get treated like 'em! We'll be closin' up until ye can learn to behave!"

Bonnie winced, understanding what the words meant. The dispensary would not be dispensing anything, and she would have to return home empty-handed, unable to a damned thing to ease her cousin's suffering. Perhaps, it would better if she just lay there on the cold, hard ground and let the storm wash over her.

Grumbles of dissent made their way up and down the line as people dispersed in a more civil fashion, abandoning the queue that they would have stomped on a helpless woman to stay in, not one minute prior.

And as the people ebbed away, Bonnie was left there on the ground, alone and in pain, unable to move, too weak to call for help, and too uncertain that anyone *would* help, even if she asked.

"I've got you," a voice said softly, as strong arms scooped her up off the pavement. "You're safe. I've got you."

Bonnie blinked to try and see the face of her white knight, but a blurry film had descended across her vision.

She could see the shape of a face but nothing more, and as the blur darkened, dragging her down into a marshy void of blackness and muffled sound, she wondered if anyone had picked her up at all, or if this was merely an angel, come to carry her soul to Heaven.

***

Bonnie woke with a start, her swollen eyelids flying open despite the thudding pain that gnawed behind her eyes.

She waited to see the familiar, rotten rafters and mildewed walls of the cottage and the vast array of cobwebs that always returned, no matter how often they were cleared, but instead she found herself staring at bright white ceilings with swan neck cornicing and an elegant ceiling rose that circled a small chandelier.

Beneath her head were soft pillows, not rolled up hessian sacks, shared with woodlice and spiders. And an eiderdown covered her to her neck, one of the feathers sticking out of the fabric, scratching at her forearm which had clearly been placed on top of the eiderdown.

"You're awake," a familiar voice gasped, as a shadow fell across her and a hand reached for hers, holding it tightly. "I was so worried. Worried twenty times over, in truth, when you didn't come to the church, and I'd heard no word from you."

Turning her stiff neck, Bonnie saw William sitting on the edge of the bed, his eyes gleaming with concern. "How... did you find me?"

"I was at the dispensary with the church folks," he explained, his voice hitching. "I almost refused, too, but I know it was divine intervention that I relented. I'd come down the line to help separate the men who were fighting, and... that's when I saw you. Why were you there, love? Why didn't you come to me? If you needed medicine, if you needed help, I would've given it freely. I would've found you a physician. I thought that's what you intended to do when you said you'd come to the church, so... I panicked when you didn't."

Bracing her hands against the soft mattress beneath her, Bonnie pushed herself into a sitting position, where dizziness swept through her pounding skull.

She squeezed her eyes shut against the rush of pain it brought with it, but she could not linger in a soft bed, not when Christopher needed her. "My cousin... He needs silver nitrate or... saltpetre. I... have to find some for him. I have to leave," she croaked, crawling towards the edge of the bed. "He has... scarlet fever. I shouldn't be here. I might have... brought the miasma with me. You might... get sick. Please, I must leave."

William hurried around to the other side of the bed and knelt before her, holding onto her hands as he peered up into her eyes. "You must recover first, my love. You have been gravely injured. I will tend to Christopher and the rest of your family. I will bring them here.

All you need do is tell me where they are, and I will fetch them."

"It is catching, my darling," Bonnie pleaded, tears stinging her eyes. "Do not put yourself in harm's way for me. I can manage. I have managed for this long, and I must do this for them. They are waiting for me."

She tried to get up, but a slam of pain ricocheted between her temples, toppling her back down onto the mattress. Her hands gripped William's like a vice, her fortitude finally failing her after months of enduring alone.

"I will take the risk. I would take any risk for you, Bonnie," William insisted, as he caught her face in his hands and pressed a kiss to her lips. "If you've brought the fevered air with you, then there's nothing you or I can do to chase it away, so what use is there in you punishing yourself by trying to proceed alone? Let me shoulder your burden now, my love; I beg of you. Let me begin to make amends for taking so long to find you."

Weeping, she clung to him, grazing her mouth against his, allowing herself to accept the warmth and love and security of him that she had craved for months.

Since the flood, she had forced herself to be strong no matter what, convinced that nobody was going to save her or her family other than herself. Yet, there he was, promising to take care of her, promising the start of a new life, and as she kissed him and held him and thanked him, she finally let herself crumble.

"I love you," William whispered, cradling the back of her head.

Bonnie mustered a tiny smile against his neck as she melted into his embrace. "I love you, too," she murmured, pressing the words onto his skin. "Goodness, how I have missed you."

At last, she could admit it.

Chapter Seventeen

Over a week had passed since Bonnie had awoken in what she now knew to be William's pleasant apartments, above a charming tailor's shop in the centre of the town, where the cathedral bells tolled the hour and pigeons cooed on the windowsill.

True to his word, William had taken his horse and cart and gone to fetch everyone from the mouldering cottage, following the detailed instructions that Bonnie had given him. Nevertheless, she had not been able to rest until she had heard the voices of her family, being led into the apartments by her beloved.

After that, a physician had been sent for, to tend to Bonnie's injuries and Christopher's affliction. A better physician than Doctor Tucker, or so it seemed, for though Christopher still wailed and writhed through days and nights of terrible fever, the redness had slowly started to fade from his skin and his tongue, once dotted with white spots, resembling a strawberry, had begun to return to normal.

He swallowed water, dripped into his mouth with a cloth, and managed to keep soup in his stomach by a similar fashion, but Bonnie would not stop praying for his survival until his fever broke and his smile and laughter returned.

As the cathedral gonged two o'clock in the morning, Bonnie glanced to the figures in the bed beside her: Alice and their mother, sound asleep.

Annabelle was in the smaller bedchamber down the hall with Christopher, while William had taken to sleeping on the settee in the parlour.

Slipping out of bed, in need of some distraction other than rest—for she had done nothing *but* rest since her encounter with the soles of people's shoes—she padded out into the hallway, wondering where to go. The door that led downstairs to the shop drew her eye and, before she knew it, she was making her way to that secret realm of industry.

The workshop and the shop itself were smaller than her father's had been, but warmer and unfettered by the memories of what had been taken from her dear father and their family.

There were no vivid bolts of silk and satin and muslin and cotton, either, just shades of black and navy and dark green, with the occasional reem of burgundy, to create the tailored garments of Sheffield's gentlemen. Still, the smell was familiar: warm and somewhat dusty, like blankets taken out of a cupboard.

"I miss you, Papa," she whispered, running her fingertips across the long workbench, not yet chipped and worn by years of toil.

She closed her eyes, imagining the beautiful gowns, exquisite tailcoats, beautiful ladies, handsome gentlemen, and the bright colours that had been a part of her life for six-and-ten years. She pictured her father humming to himself as he wandered back and forth between bolts of fabric, cutting through them with his long, sharp scissors, knowing precisely how much he needed without having to measure. She imagined him hunched over his workbench, sewing beads and lace and embroidering the most detailed flowers and vines.

His talent had been unmatched, and to think that his legacy had been so viciously tarnished ached like an old wound in her heart.

Sitting on the high stool of the workbench, Bonnie reached for a few scraps of burgundy fabric and, taking out her needle and borrowing some thread, she began to sew. At first, she did not know what she intended to make, but as her hands moved, weaving the thread through the fabric, a tiny dress began to form.

I'll put it on a wooden spoon, she thought, *and make an ornament of it.*

Hard at work, concentrating upon the seams of the miniature gown, Bonnie did not realise that she was being watched from the doorway of the workshop. She did not hear the soft footsteps making their way across the stone floor, nor feel the presence of William until he was sitting beside her.

Yet, she did not jump in fright at the sight of him, for in his apartments, in his world, she had started to feel safe again, no longer petrified of someone bursting through the cottage's makeshift door and throwing everyone out.

"It's a little small for you, don't you think?" he said, laughing softly.

Bonnie cast him a sideways glance. "It's practice. I wanted to see if I remembered how."

"It's in your blood, Bonnie," William told her. "I doubt you could forget, even if you wanted to."

She sighed. "Never has a truer word been spoken." She gestured at the workshop. "I haven't had time to miss somewhere like this, but now that I'm here—it's all rushing back, and I wonder if it was more bearable when I didn't have a moment to think of... everything. Papa would've been so proud of you, if he could see this, if he could see all you've done for his family."

"He'd have cursed my name if he'd ever discovered that I worked for Mr. Shannon," William argued. "I curse myself for not seeing the truth. He sabotaged those gowns, you know?"

Bonnie nodded. "I know."

"He took pride in telling his apprentices what he had done," William continued sombrely. "I wanted to wring his neck when he admitted it for the first time, and... I believe that was when I decided I was going to take the bolt of silk and come to you, long before the flood made the decision final for me. But, there's some fortunate news."

Bonnie raised an eyebrow. "There is?"

"His business is floundering," William replied. "His gowns are flimsy and unfashionable, and he never got his hands on your father's designs— your mother burned them, the morning of your departure. Already, he has lines outside the door of complaining patrons, demanding recompense. I don't think it'll be long before he has to give up, if he hasn't already."

A smile tugged at the corners of Bonnie's lips. "I do enjoy a comeuppance, and Mr. Shannon is long overdue for one."

"I couldn't agree more." He leaned closer, his arm against hers. "But I have to ask something, Bonnie."

She frowned. "What, love?"

"Do you forgive me?"

She coughed out a chuckle. "I do, my darling. I didn't understand before, what it takes to keep those you love alive. Your mother wasn't well, she needed medicine, and you no longer had employment. You did what you needed to do, and I would've done the same in your situation, now that I've seen what desperation looks and feels like." She paused. "How *is* your mother?"

"Living like a queen with my aunt, by the sea," William answered, laughing. "I don't think she misses me at all."

Bonnie batted him on the arm. "I doubt that very much."

"Well, she'd miss my income, but that's it," he teased, turning in his seat. "She'll be pleased when I finally write to her to tell her I'm to be married, though."

Bonnie smiled. "Oh, and who is the fortunate lady?"

"Well, I've not asked her yet—not properly, anyway," he said, lifting his hand to her face, stroking his thumb across the apple of her cheek. "So, Bonnie Acklam, do you think you might do me the greatest honour and consent to be my wife?"

Bonnie hesitated, lowering her gaze as reality dawned like a black cloud scudding across the sun. "I love you, William. I have loved you for the longest time, but... I'm not the same woman you knew in York." Her breath hitched. "There's much of me that has been ruined, there are parts of me that will be healed and parts of me that won't, and... though I love you dearly, I don't know if you'll still love the woman I've become. I'm not sure if I'm worthy of it."

"Nonsense," he told her gently. "I have loved you since I was a boy. I have loved so many iterations of you, and it would be my greatest privilege to love the many iterations of you that are still to come. My feelings haven't changed, nor will they, but, I promise you, even if you don't want me as a husband, my home is yours.

Of course, I would rather be your husband, but—"

She kissed him, looping her arms around his neck and pulling him close. His lips were frozen in surprise for a moment, but as his arm slipped around her waist, holding her against him in kind, he kissed her back: soft and slow and hopeful, like a prayer or a promise, sealed between them.

Pulling back, Bonnie opened her mouth to answer, when someone else's voice filled the sweet silence that she had intended to.

"Bonnie, William, hurry!" Alice yelped from the workshop doorway. "It's Christopher—his fever has broken!"

And though Bonnie was only just recovering her faith in fate and wishes, she flashed William a grin, certain that it was because of him and the vow he made a year ago that fortune was beginning smile on her and her family once more. *He* was the wish she had made, and it was slowly coming true.

NELL HARTE

Epilogue

Summer, York 1867

"It's crooked, isn't it?" William swept a hand through his silky, golden-brown hair; his brow glistening with sweat, his face spattered with paint.

Bonnie tilted her head, resting it upon his shoulder. "I don't think so."

"Well, you won't see it straight, looking at it that way," he chided playfully, turning his head to kiss the top of her head. "I should've asked someone to do it for me."

Bonnie slipped her arm around her husband's waist. "I think it looks wonderful, my love. Perfect, actually."

In pale grey writing, set upon a forest green background, the sign above the shop read: *Acklam & Greaves, Fine Tailoring and Dressmakers.* Although, anyone with a pressing need for ballroom attire already knew precisely where to find them, for in the two-and-a-half years since they had been reunited, the married pair had become quite famous for their prized garments.

At first, Bonnie had refused any suggestion that she should pick up her dressmaking talents where she had left off, feeling it was somehow a betrayal to her father. But as ladies had begun to come into the shop in Sheffield, asking if William also made gowns, she had agreed to make just one to see how it felt.

As it turned out, it had been like tasting freedom after years incarcerated, her recovered hands and restored spirits taking back the reins of imagination and creativity that she had thought she had lost.

"Is it strange?" William asked, resting his cheek upon her hair.

Bonnie shrugged. "Yes and no. I would be lying if I said I thought we'd ever come back to York, so to return to the place where I grew up, reclaiming everything that was taken... it isn't not strange."

"But you're happy?" He sounded anxious.

She smiled. "Blissfully. Even Annabelle has decided she doesn't mind the bells of York Minster anymore."

A few months prior, William had received word from Mr. Penwortham that the old shop had become available again, following the colossal failure of Mr. Shannon's enterprise. It seemed likely that Mr. Penwortham had also seen the success of Mr. and Mrs. Greaves in the papers, for wherever there was a ball or a gathering, there was mention of their fine gowns and tailored garments.

With more than enough income from the Sheffield shop to move back to York, the happy couple had made the decision without delay, carting everyone back to the city that meant so much to the Acklams.

Clara and Alice had adjusted as if they had never left, though Clara took longer to get up and down the stairs than she once had. Meanwhile, Annabelle had taken a dislike to the city for the first month, before finding employment as a housemaid to one of the patrons of the shop.

Since then, she had been besotted with York, returning to the shop every Sunday to tell stories of what she had seen and heard all week.

As for Christopher, he was as cheerful a child as any who was safe and loved, and though he had recovered from the scarlet fever that had held him in its grip, he had not emerged from the sickness without consequence.

The scarlet fever had left him blind in one eye, and mostly blind in the other, but he did not seem to mourn the loss of his sight. Being so young, he adapted, and beyond a few accidental bruises from knocking into walls and furniture, he could not have been happier and everyone who came into the shop and saw him loved to dote upon him.

Indeed, there were moments when Bonnie would watch him making his way through the apartments as if he had no loss of sight at all, knowing the rooms so well that he rarely made a misstep.

Just then, Alice poked her head out of the shop's entrance. "Will you be much longer? Mama says the stew will thicken too much if the pair of you don't hurry to the table, and I can't wait a moment longer to have some of the cake." She paused as another voice drifted down to the street.

"Tell 'em I didn't put all me patience into that cake so they could stand out there, lookin' like love itself all day! It's not often I get to celebrate me birthday with people I like!"

Bonnie grinned, her heart swelling with contentment at the sound of Dora's voice. The older woman had followed the family to York upon Bonnie's invitation, after explaining that Clara needed a companion and a housekeeper and a cook, and that Bonnie needed her dear friend to be nearby.

Dora, weary after so many years at the steelworks, had accepted without hesitation, filling the apartments with chatter and laughter and a joy that had made Clara smile more than she had done in years.

In truth, the two older women had become thick as thieves, always hobbling off to the inn at the bottom of the road of an evening and coming back later in the night, cackling raucously.

"We're coming!" Bonnie shouted up to the open window of the apartments.

Dora stuck her head out, grinning. "Aye, thought that might get yer backsides up them stairs!" She craned her neck. "The sign's crooked."

"I told you," William grumbled, sighing.

But Bonnie just peered up at him, smiling. "And I told you it's perfect. I think I like it more *because* it's crooked, because the path for us to get here hasn't exactly been straight, now, has it?"

"How is it that you can always see the good in things?" He chuckled, turning to cradle her face, tucking the loose strands of hair behind her ears.

"Someone taught me that I could do anything," she replied, pressing her palms to his chest, feeling his steady heartbeat. "Someone reminded me of my strength, and as long as we keep that strength, I'm sure we can survive the shame of some slightly crooked letters."

Alice cleared her throat. "If you're going to start kissing, I'm going upstairs, and I'm going to throw a bucket of water out of the window."

"We're coming," Bonnie insisted, laughing.

Taking her husband's hand, she led him back into the cool shade of the shop and closed the door behind them. William twisted the key in the lock and turned the small sign that read "closed," so they would not be disturbed.

With that, they headed up the stairs to the apartments that had changed so much, yet not at all.

There were, of course, more people to occupy the rooms, but it was an alteration that Bonnie cherished. With Christopher and Dora and, on Sundays, Annabelle, there was never a quiet moment to allow the ghosts of the past to slip through the cracks and make the apartments feel sad again.

There were days of memory, to mourn those who were no longer there, but with the burden carried upon more shoulders, the grief was less heavy upon their hearts.

"There they are!" Dora scolded lightly, ushering everyone into their chairs around the kitchen table.

"Don't start without me!" a voice wailed, as footsteps thundered up the stairs and a blur darted into the room. Panting, Annabelle took her seat at the table, dabbing the sweat from her brow with her sleeve. "I told Mrs. Sutcliffe that I would collect her gown, so she let me come here for the evenin'. Doesn't matter if it's not finished; she won't get rid of me, considering you make all of her dresses."

Bonnie leaned over and pressed a kiss to Annabelle's forehead. "Now, everything really *is* perfect. Everyone is here."

As Dora served the rich, meaty stew and oven-warmed rolls of fresh bread, and the mismatched family began to eat and talk and joke and laugh, marvelling at the little songs that Christopher had made up, Bonnie found her husband's hand underneath the table and held it tight, squeezing it to say, *"How lucky we are, my love. How very, very lucky."*

It was something that Bonnie would never allow herself to forget, for she now knew how quickly good fortune could be snatched away, and though she hoped they had received all of their misfortune for a lifetime, she knew there were others who were struggling out in the world. As such, every other evening, she and William went to the church to feed the needy, and would continue to do so until there was not a hungry mouth left to feed.

But, for just that moment, she allowed herself to savour their luck and comfort and happiness, finally back where she belonged, surrounded by people she loved, but never forgetting those they had lost.

"To our family," she said suddenly, raising her glass.

"To our family," everyone chorused back, clinking the glasses together, while Christopher attempted to toast with a bread roll.

William leaned in, whispering close to her ear, "To you, my darling. To us. To love."

"To all of that and more," she replied, kissing his cheek. *Indeed, to many more days like this one,* she added secretly, for every day that passed was her happiest yet, and she would never take another one for granted.

The End

I hope that you enjoyed this book.

If you are willing to leave a short and honest review for me on Amazon, it will be very much appreciated, as reviews help to get my books noticed.

Subscribe here to receive Nell Harte's newsletter.

Over the page you will find a preview of one of my other books

The Little Orphan's Christmas Miracle

VICTORIAN ROMANCE

THE LITTLE ORPHAN'S
Christmas Miracle

NELL HARTE

PREVIEW

The Little Orphan's Christmas Miracle

Nell Harte

Chapter One

London

1852

The carollers had all gone home, the Christmas Eve dinners had all been eaten, the wreaths had all been frozen stiff on the doorways, the Nativity scenes were all slumbering in dark living rooms, the sun had been gone for a very long time, the kisses had been exchanged under the mistletoe, and the whole city of London had fallen dark and silent as though it was any other morning.

The grand new clock tower that people called Big Ben tolled out four long, sonorous notes. Its sound was almost the only sound in the entire city, except for the shriek of the wind around corners and under eaves, rattling every one of the small, squinting windows of the workhouse.

Even on a street as poor as this one, Christmas could still be found. The church on the corner was all lit up with candles, every surface bedecked in ribbons and holly, great drapes of mistletoe hanging on the backs of every pew.

It seemed as though the day's carols still hung somewhere in the rafters of the church. Up and down and across the street, too, stockings hung on mantelpieces and wreaths bumped and crunched on doors, every leaf edged with a pure white border of frost.

But in the workhouse itself, deep inside its dank halls, hiding in the women's dormitory that at that moment echoed with screams, in the heart of the old matron crouched at the foot of one of the narrow beds, Christmas was something that had perished a long, long time ago.

"Stop your noise, girl," growled Rosalyn West. "You'll wake the whole house."

In response, the girl that sat on the bed with her knees drawn up to her chest let out a long, keening moan against gritted teeth. A slip of a girl, she was. Her shoulders jutted hopelessly against the rough cloth of her white nightgown. Her cheeks were scarlet, sweat trickling down them as she panted. How old was she? Sixteen? Seventeen? If that.

Mrs. West pulled back the hem of the nightgown for a better view. "The baby's crowning. You'll need to push soon."

"I can't," sobbed the girl. She fell back against the pillows, her fingertips white where they clutched her legs just below the knees. "I can't push anymore."

Mrs, West resisted the urge to rub her burning eyes. "We don't want to be here all night," she barked.

The girl raised her weary head and looked around at the silent audience that surrounded her. Every woman in the workhouse was staring. She glanced at Mrs. West's face, as though to ask for a little privacy, but then another long, shuddering contraction gripped her body, making her curl in half and let out a primal shriek.

"Push. Push!" barked Mrs. West.

The girl's scream rose to an inhuman pitch, her toes curling deep into the straw mattress, and a rush of fluid gushed over the bed. The babe's face appeared, scrunched up, purple and blue. Perhaps it would be dead. It would be better, in a way, if the child was dead.

The mother was sobbing. "I can't. I can't. I have no strength left." Her fingers were starting to go limp.

"You can't give up now," Mrs. West ordered. "One more push. One more *good* push."

"No. No, I don't have it in me." The girl's tears mingled with sweat and soaked into her nightgown. "Make it stop. Please, please, please, make it stop." Her sobs were desperate and childlike now. Begging.

Mrs. West glared at the girl. What was her name? It took her a few moments to remember. Joanna. Joanna Gray.

"Joanna," she snapped. "Open your eyes."

Joanna did so, more out of the long habit of dreading obedience than anything else.

"You shall push. Now." Mrs. West reached for a towel and held it out, ready. "Or you and your child will both be dead before the hour is out."

Joanna's eyes widened in terror. Another contraction washed through her body, and she threw back her head and screamed, a raw and hoarse and despairing sound, and her entire body curled. The baby was shooting towards Mrs. West then, a rush of blood and fluid and purplish skin.

She caught it, wrapped the blanket around it and lifted it from the soaked bedclothes.

Joanna fell back, her limp arms collapsing on either side of the narrow bed, and for a moment Mrs. West was certain the girl was dead.

It was at that moment that a feeble cry rose from the bundle in her arms. She looked down to see that the babe was not dead after all. Tiny fists were outstretched on arms thinner than a man's fingers, and the little mouth was wide open, colour flushing into the baby's face as it screamed, drawing frigid air into tiny lungs for the first time.

For a few seconds, Mrs. West felt something other than the chaos of roaring pain that had been tearing her apart for so very long. At that moment she was no longer an exhausted and angry widow crouched on a cold workhouse floor, holding a baby that no one had planned and nobody wanted.

She was a young mother herself, although not as young as this one, sitting up in a warm and clean bed, holding in her arms a baby that she had longed for since she could remember. She looked down not into the face of this emaciated, undersized baby, but into the face of the baby she herself had prayed for, for so many years.

And she was not in a great workhouse dormitory surrounded by desperate women, but in a bedroom with a midwife washing her hands in the corner and, beside her, a man whose eyes were filled with love and pride.

Then, Joanna Gray sat up, sucking in a long and desperate breath, clawing her way back to life. She reached out, her pale eyes crazed, as though the sound of that cry had awakened her from the brink of death. "Give it to me," she croaked. "Give it."

Mrs. West looked into the girl's eyes and saw not maternal love but a fierce, base instinct clawing to the surface. She held out the baby, and the girl grabbed it awkwardly, and as it was lifted from Mrs. West's arms, it was as though it was all happening again.

Driving home from church that Sunday, laughing together. Little Miss West's eyes round and bright. Mr. West at the reins, his smile wide. The out-of-control brewers' dray barrelling around the corner. There had been splintering wood, screaming, and a terrible, terrible silence. A silence that followed widowed, childless Mrs. West into this very room, into the centre of her very heart.

Mrs. West did not scream or cry. There was no point. She had screamed and cried until it seemed her very spirit had been poured out of her along with her voice. She cut the cord, covered up the new mother, wrapped a clean towel around the baby.

She moved Joanna and the child onto the next bed and stripped the soiled one. She stood over them both, amazed that they were alive, this young woman whose ribs showed plainly under her skin as she fed the baby, this infant whose fingers and toes were blue already with the pervasive cold that seeped into the stones of the warehouse.

How was it that these two were alive, when her dear John and her sweet Anna were dead?

Joanna closed her eyes and leaned her head back against the pillow, her arms limp around the baby.

"What's the child's name?" Mrs. West asked.

Joanna's eyes opened. "What?"

"You have to name the child. I must write it down in the ledger and arrange for the christening." Mrs. West snorted a little, looking away at that last word. As if this wretch deserved such grace. The irony that she herself deserved no grace, that perhaps nobody did, that perhaps that was the very nature of grace, did not occur to her.

"Oh, I... I..." Joanna looked down, parted the blankets slightly. "A girl," she breathed. "A little girl." She stared down at the baby as though it was the whole world.

"A name," snapped Mrs. West.

Joanna raised fevered eyes upon the world and gazed through the one tiny window of the room. The church was just visible, all lit up with candlelight, a wreath hanging from the door.

"It's Christmas," she said, surprised.

"Yes." Mrs. West folded her arms.

Joanna was silent for a long moment, staring at the baby. "I have no family name to give you," she whispered, tracing a finger along the tiny cheek. "So let's name you something happy. Something Christmassy."

Mrs. West waited without patience.

"Holly." Joanna looked up. "Holly Gray. That's my baby's name."

Mrs. West nodded briefly and turned to leave.

Let's name you something happy.

A pathetic attempt, she thought, at believing that Christmas meant anything and that this little girl's life would be anything but misery.

* * * *

Mrs. West had slept barely an hour when she had to rise again, wake the inmates, bully the staff into getting their breakfast ready, and start the day. A day like any other, until she flung wide the workhouse door and heard the lively sound of the church choir singing "Joy to the World" in the church next door. The sound sickened her. What joy was there in this world, she wondered, looking up and down the bleak and grey street? What joy was there in a world that could take everything from you in one heartbeat, in one collision, in one fell swoop?

She was the one who had wanted to take that route home from church that morning.

The wind was freezing. She was grateful for its howl in her ears as she walked down the short path to the gate of the workhouse grounds; it drowned out some of the Christmas carol. She unlocked the gate with a giant key on a heavy iron ring, but before she could turn back into the workhouse, a voice reached her ears.

"Hallooo, Mrs. West! Wait!"

She looked up. The familiar figure of a cheerful, portly policeman was strutting up the street towards her, and she groaned inwardly. The last thing she wanted to do this morning was to deal with happy people.

Happiness grated on her pain, like salt in a wound. And Constable Joey Mitchell was one of the happiest people she knew. His jolly red cheeks were, as always, squashed by a wide smile; a tumult of golden curls peeked out from under his hat, and, to her immense disgust, he was towing a very small boy along by the arm.

The boy was one of the scruffiest children that Mrs. West had ever seen, and she had seen a good many scruffy children. The tiny bones in his thin arms jutted against pale skin stretched tight over his frame, as though he had nothing to spare, not even skin.

His eyes were deeply buried in great hollows in his face, and they were a brown so dark they were almost completely black, like great pits of need staring up at her. Though he could not have been more than three years old, his black hair hung in awful mats, reaching just beneath his chin.

An oversized shirt hung from his bony frame, covered with holes, and his tiny feet were bare. He had two toes missing on each foot, the little toe and the one beside it. Frostbite, Mrs. West knew, without having to ask; some of the skin was still blackened. She wondered how he had survived this long.

"Found this little chap wanderin' around all on his own, like," bubbled the constable. "Told him you'd take good care of him, didn't I, little man?"

The boy regarded them both speechlessly. His tears were washing down his neck, black with dirt.

"Good morning, constable," said Mrs. West stiffly. "Where did you find him?"

"Oh, down by the slums, poor mite. Scratchin' around in the rubbish for something to eat." Joey beamed at her. "He'll be safe with you."

"I'm afraid so," Mrs. West sighed. "Do you know his name?"

"He says it's Theodore and he can't find his mam. I'd wager he's been abandoned." He ruffled the boys head "Theodore's quite a big name for such a little chap, isn't it?"

The child continued to cry, slowly and continuously, as though he had been crying for as long as he could remember.

"I suppose he has to come in, then," said Mrs. West with distaste. She held open the gate. "Come on."

Theodore hesitated.

"Run along, lad." Joey disentangled his hand from the boy's and gave him a friendly little shove. "Mrs. West will take care of you."

Theodore stared up at her for a long moment. Then, shoulders slumping, he shuffled through the gate.

She slammed it behind him. "Good day to you," she said to Joey.

Joey grinned and doffed his hat. "Merry Christmas, Mrs. West!"

Mrs. West gripped the boy by the arm and marched him up to the workhouse. No day could be merry in which she had two more mouths to feed.

And to Mrs. West, there was no Christmas.

Chapter Two

Four Years Later

A piece of straw was poking into Holly's cheek. She brushed at it, giggling when it tickled across her nose.

"Hush," Mama's voice whispered. A cold hand gripped her arm. "Hush, Holly."

Holly sneezed. She knew it was wrong when Mama had told her to hush, but she couldn't help it.

"Holly!" Mama hissed. "Be quiet."

Holly opened her eyes. Mama's pinched, pale face hovered in front of her. Her own skinny back was pressed against the wall; her head was pillowed on Mama's arm. Mama shifted uncomfortably, and the bed squeaked as the other woman who shared it with them – Rhonda – rolled over. She was bigger than Mama, and shoved her effortlessly against Holly; Mama braced her hands on the wall to keep Holly from getting squashed.

"I'm sorry, Mama," Holly whispered.

"Shhh. Please, poppet. Just go back to sleep," Mama breathed. She hooked a strand of hair out of Holly's face. "It's not morning yet."

Holly obediently closed her eyes and nuzzled against Mama's chest. Mama stroked her hair, which she loved very much. Her tummy was aching with hunger.

"Mama?" she whispered.

"Holly, please." Mama closed her eyes, her head sinking onto the straw. "Just be quiet a little longer."

"All right." Holly paused. "I'm hungry."

"Yes. We all are. But hush now."

It was too late. The bed creaked as Rhonda sat up, her eyes glaring down at Mama and Holly through slitted lids, a red pattern on her cheek where it had been pressed against the straw.

"Silence that brat," she growled, "or I'll do it myself."

"Yes, Rhonda, of course." Mama cowered against Holly, wrapping her in her arms. "I'm sorry. It won't happen again."

"It better not," snarled Rhonda. She sank back onto the straw mattress, giving Mama a cruel thump with her elbow as she did so, not quite by accident.

Holly cuddled against Mama, feeling sorry that she had woken Rhonda, but she couldn't say so because Rhonda would be angry again. She wished people would stop being angry with Mama. Mama was the whole world. With a small finger, she traced the curve of Mama's cheek.

Normally, this would make Mama smile a little bit. Instead, now, she squeezed her eyes shut a little tighter, and a teardrop squeezed out of one eye and ran down her nose.

Mama cried a lot. Holly wished she would smile a little bit more, and she didn't understand why her touch wasn't working like it always did. She cuddled against her body and closed her eyes.

It felt like seconds later that the breakfast bell was clanging and Rhonda was leaping out of bed, elbowing the other women out of the way as they headed for the breakfast hall. Holly sat up, grabbing Mama's hand. "Mama, Mama, wake up!" she said. "It's Christmas! It's Christmas!"

Mama sat up very slowly, tears running down her cheeks. Holly couldn't understand. The other women had been talking about Christmas for weeks. Holly wasn't exactly sure what it was, only that she had a vague memory of excitement from a long time ago, and today everyone was chattering about it. They said that there wouldn't be any work – Mama hated work, even though Holly tried to help – and the women had talked about a special dinner, with enough food for everyone, which Holly hadn't known was a possibility.

Christmas sounded perfect. Why was Mama sad about it?

"Mama, what wrong?" Holly gripped Mama's sleeve and stared up at her.

"Nothing, love." Mama wiped at her tears, then scooped Holly into her arms. "Sit with me just a little while before we wash up and go to breakfast."

Holly squirmed. "But Mama, I'm hungry."

"I know. I know. But just give me two minutes more," Mama breathed. She held Holly against her chest, pressing her nose into Holly's neck and taking a deep breath as though she liked the smell. "Just two minutes more," she whispered.

Holly leaned her head against Mama's shoulder and closed her eyes, wrapping her small fists in the matted locks of her mother's hair. They sat together like that for a few seconds, just breathing. Holly could feel the thud of Mama's heart against her cheek.

The breakfast bell rang again, and Holly sat up. "Mama, I'm hungry!"

"I know, I know." Mama got up and tried to smile, but it was as though her face wasn't quite working right. She gripped Holly's hand. "Come on. Let's go and get breakfast."

They went to the small, frigid washroom, where Mama splashed cold water on Holly's face and tried to clean the tears from her own. Then, following a hallway as long and black as a tunnel, they went through to the dining hall.

"Look, my love." Mama pointed. "All the pretty decorations are for Christmas!"

Holly looked up, a burst of excitement rushed through her. Garlands hung all around the dining hall, punctuated by sprigs of bright holly, their berries brilliantly red. There was a little bunting here and there, too, and when Holly took a deep breath, she smelled something that rarely ever passed her lips: sugar.

Her mouth fell open, and she turned this way and that, staring at it all.

Perhaps the mistletoe was a bit wilted, perhaps the bunting was grubby and hung limp, perhaps the holly berries were rather wrinkled and the sugar was only a few pinches to season the dry porridge they always had for breakfast – but it was new and it was different and Holly could barely remember ever seeing anything new and different in the dining hall before.

"Oh, Mama!" she gasped. "It's pretty!"

Mama was wiping away a tear. "Yes, lovey. It's very pretty."

Holly frowned, reaching up to Mama's cheek. "Mama, why are you crying?"

"Don't worry about that." Mama smiled. "Come on. Let's have some of that porridge."

There was a tiny bit of milk for the porridge, too, and Holly bounced around Mama's knees in excitement as she walked to one of the long thin tables with two tin bowls steaming in her hands. They always sat in the furthest corner of the dining hall, away from the other women, and today was no different. Mama lifted Holly onto a bench as hard as a bone and set the bowl in front of her. "Eat it slowly now, darling," she said. "Or you'll make yourself sick."

She gave Holly a tin spoon. Sniffing with delight at the sweet, creamy scent of this new porridge – she had eaten porridge every morning that she could remember, but could never remember eating it with sugar and milk like this before – she scooped up a spoonful and shoveled it into her mouth. The sweetness burst wonderfully on her tongue.

"Mama!" she cried, mouth full.

"Shhh." Mama stroked her hair. Her own porridge was untouched. "Don't speak with your mouth full."

Holly decided against speaking at all and ate the rest of the porridge in giant gulps, even though Mama kept telling her to slow down. Christmas, she decided, was wonderful. Christmas was bunting in the dining hall and porridge with sugar for breakfast. She was sure she had never had a day as glorious as this before in her life.

When Mama had picked her way through her own oats, she took Holly by the hand and led her up to the front of the dining hall to place their bowls in a huge tin tub. Sometimes Mama and Holly would help with the washing-up, but today it was two other women's turn to do so. They glared sourly at Holly as she stood on tiptoe to place her bowl in the tub. Holly looked up at them, wondering if they even knew it was Christmas. Perhaps she should tell them.

"Merry Christmas," she said.

The stouter of the two women growled and drew back a hand as if to strike her. Holly cringed, but the other woman put a hand on her companion's arm, stopping her.

"Leave the child," she said. "Today it's her birthday you know, she will be four years old." She gave the other woman a meaningful look.

The stouter woman's eyes flickered. She looked away, and Mama tugged on Holly's arm, leading her forward.

"Today's my birthday, Mama?" Holly asked, looking up at her mother.

"Yes, darling." Mama's voice trembled, and when Holly saw where she was staring, she immediately understood why.

Mrs. West was standing in the dining hall doorway.

Holly's stomach seemed to turn a slow somersault inside her belly, making a prickle of cold sweat start on the back of her neck and the palms of her hands. There was nothing in her universe more terrifying than Mrs. West. She was massive, towering over everything, her black eyes lost in the craggy folds of her unforgiving face. Her body looked as hard and immovable as though every part of her had been carved from granite, particularly her jutting lower jaw, and Holly knew from experience that those hands, fastened upon one's ear or applied sharply to one's cheek or buttock, were harder and colder than stone could ever be.

"Gray," Mrs. West growled.

Holly trembled. Gray was the name that Mrs. West always called Mama, although the other women always called her Joanna. Nothing good ever happened when Mrs. West called to Mama.

Mama's hand clenched over Holly's, hard and cold, grinding the small bones in her little hand together.

"Ow," Holly whimpered.

Mama dragged herself before Mrs. West like a prisoner thrown before a merciless judge. "Yes?" she whispered.

"Don't make a fuss now," Mrs. West said shortly. "You know it will do no good. Hand over the child and let's not make it unpleasant."

Mama stood shivering for a long, long moment, and the tears continued to pour down her cheeks. Holly didn't understand. Why was Mama crying? What did *hand over* mean? Was Mrs. West talking about her?

"Mrs. West, please," Mama choked out. "Please."

"You know the rules." Mrs. West held out one hand. "It's this or the streets, Gray."

Mama gripped Holly's hand even tighter. The shock of pain and the sight of Mama's tears made Holly wail, and she felt her own tears burning her eyes.

"She's my baby," Mama said. "She's my baby. Don't take her. You can't take her."

"I think you'll find that I can. You forfeited your right to a family when you came here."

"I was pregnant and starving. I was desperate. There was no other way for her to survive." Mama was sobbing now. "How can you do this? How can you take a child away from her mother?"

Away? Holly let out a shriek, clutching Mama's arm. "Mama! Mama!"

"Enough!" barked Mrs. West. She stepped forward, grabbing Holly's arm. Holly shrieked at the top of her lungs.

"No!" Mama screamed. "No, no, no, no!" Her voice was high and wild now, unnatural, a bird's cry, and her grip on Holly's hand felt like it was going to crush her. But Mrs. West was pulling too now, and she was grabbing Mama's arm and shouting, and the other women were running up to her.

"Let me go!" Mama yelled. Her eyes were wide and wild. "LET ME GO!"

Holly screamed and screamed, her piercing voice ripping through the air, the sound burning her throat. Mama was sobbing, her grip failing, and then Holly's arm shot through Mama's and Mrs. West snatched her up by the arm. The movement wrenched Holly's shoulder, and she shrieked again, but Mrs. West tucked her under her arm and no amount of screaming or pummelling with her wrists could get her free. Two other women had grabbed Mama by the arms, and she was throwing herself against them like a wild animal.

"To the refractory ward with her!" Mrs. West trumpeted.

"No. No. NO!" Mama shrieked.

Holly howled with all of her might, but she was powerless to make any of it stop. She was just a little girl trapped under Mrs. West's iron arm, screaming as her mother was dragged away to the refractory ward, to some place that swallowed her, never to be seen again.

READ THE REST

Printed in Great Britain
by Amazon